SADDLE TRAMP #20

SHELTER

BY PAUL LEDD

McG's
BOOK STORE
910 S. LOOP 494
PORTER, TX. 77365

ZEBRA BOOKS
KENSINGTON PUBLISHING CORP.

ZEBRA BOOKS

are published by

Kensington Publishing Corp.
475 Park Avenue South
New York, N.Y. 10016

Copyright © 1984 by Kensington Publishing Corp.

All rights reserved. No part of this book may be reproduced in any form or by any means without the prior written consent of the Publisher, excepting brief quotes used in reviews.

First printing: October 1984

Printed in the United States of America

1.

She was a big woman and when Lola Allison moved across a room men's eyes painted her with lustful wishes. She was a blonde, nearly six feet tall with breasts like ripe melons soft and challenging, with long tapered thighs and a slim waist, cool green eyes, a broad mouth made to devour a man.

That was just what Shelter Morgan had in mind.

He sat on the ege of the hotel bed watching Lola as she moved through the last stages of divestment. It was an art with Lola and Shelter sat watching with rapt interest and a rising pulse rate.

She lifted her long arms slowly overhead, sliding from her white silk blouse as she did so. She smiled across her shoulder at Shelter Morgan, a most appreciative audience of one. The shoes were next, slowly unbuttoned as Lola bent far forward, that broad, perfectly rounded ass turned toward Shell.

"Well?" Lola asked, raising her shoes overhead.

"Charming."

"But you do like it?" she asked sulkily. Then she stepped nearer to Shelter, looked down at him as he sat naked, waiting. "You like it," she said, immensely pleased as she studied his groin.

"Very much," Shell reassured her.

She did a little pirouette away from him and sat at the red velvet chair across the room, beside the window where dull gray light seeped in from the outside the Hogan, Colorado hotel.

She crossed her legs and began unrolling the red silk stockings she wore, humming all the time, her head cocked brightly toward Shell, her green eyes growing soft and sensual.

She stood again and as he watched, she peeled off her chemise in one easy, rapid motion and stood there naked, open to inspection. Shelter let his eyes sweep up her inch by inch, taking in the lines of her legs, the soft inner thighs, pale and smooth as ivory, the softly rounded belly with the round, concave navel, the well-structured rib cage which supported the jutting, glorious breasts. Those breasts! Proud, outthrust, as remarkable and shapely unsupported as they had been peering from behind the red satin of the dancehall girl's costume. Looking at their smooth expanse made Shell's hands ache; studying the pink budding nipples made his mouth water.

He focused lastly on the dark, downy nest between her thighs, wanting to bury his hands and face there, to shove that slowly, heavily throbbing erection deep into its sheltered nook.

"Come here," he said, his voice slightly raw.

"Ready?"

"You know damn well I am."

And he was—it had been six weeks on the trail from

California, six weeks without the company of a human being. There had been only the blue roan gelding he rode and the night dreaming of a woman such as Lola Allison.

He rolled onto his back and she came to him, moving gracefully, in measured strides. She had remarkable poise, he decided. Maybe she had been a dancer. Her steps, smooth, utterly feminine, were taken with the care of a juggler.

Shelter watched her, feeling the dryness in his throat, the need to reach out and grab her, to throw her down, spread those glorious thighs and slip in to her. He managed to keep from doing that, but just barely.

She towered over him now, her eyes combing him seductively, lingering on his crotch. He could see little sparks of delight in those eyes, delight as she looked the tall man up and down his six foot three length, studying the hard-muscled abdomen, the strong chest, the long, well-defined muscles of the thighs. She looked into those deep blue eyes, eyes which seemed utterly cold at times, at the dark hair falling across his thoughtful forehead at the dark full beard he wore now.

Lola knelt beside the bed and her hands rested on his thigh. Then she went exploring, slowly, maddeningly. Fingers ran the length of his hard shaft, toyed with the head of it, inflaming him as her breath, rapid and warm now touched his abdomen, his thighs.

She hefted his sack, cupping it in her palms like a rare thing. She bent low, ran her tongue up along his inner thigh and then her teeth nipped at him, gently, teasingly.

"Be careful there, woman," Morgan said and his hand found her mass of yellow hair, his fingers intertwining in it, searching for and finding the pink, whorled ear which he stroked gently.

Lola continued her exploring. Her lips went up

across Shelter's belly and chest, pausing to touch his small, hard nipples. Then she kissed his throat, ears, eyes before her mouth found his lips and locked on there, before her body which had slowly slid upward, across Shell's began to work against his, reaching a slow cadence.

Reaching back, Lola found Shell's erection and began to finger it, to stroke it. She kissed Shelter ardently, her body pressed tightly to his, her breath coming in short gasps.

She lifted herself, spreading her thighs as she positioned Shelter and slowly began to settle, holding herself poised for a long moment over him, without moving, without breathing before her warmth slid up and over him and she took him in with a gasp which rose from deep in her throat.

Shelter wrapped his hand in her profuse blond hair and pulled her down to him again, his mouth bruising hers, tasting each lip, taking in her darting pink tongue, flashing urgent messages to Lola who began to writhe and sway, to pitch against him, her pelvis hard against his as her dampness smeared against Shell's groin and Morgan was lifted to a hard, sudden climax.

Lola groaned and her fingers clutched at him. She sat up erectly, her head thrown back, eyes half closed, lips parted as her inner muscles made slow contracting demands.

He could feel her begin to twitch, to spasm and she suddenly collapsed against him as if her arms hadn't the strength to hold her up. She lay there gasping, Shell's hands roaming her back, her broad, smooth buttocks, his lips tasting hair and throat, neck and shoulder.

He lay there relaxed and warm. Outside the skies were gray over the mountains; the wind was wailing in the eaves, lifting the shake shingles on the mine office across the street. From time to time the walls of the hotel shook with the force of the wind. Shelter paid it no mind. He dozed peacefully, feeling the soft, sated breath of Lola against his chest, feeling her fingers clutch involuntarily at him in her sleep.

He closed his eyes and slept.

He slept and they came again with their thunder guns, with their hands dripping blood. He was there again, back along the Conasauga River in Georgia in the last days of the war . . .

"Captain Morgan?"

Shelter looked up into the face of the corporal. He was angry at having been awakened. That was the only sanctuary. Now he sat up, looking around the pitiful camp. There were burned oaks around the clearing, a few patched tents hidden among the trees. One of them was the medical tent and now and then the screams came, the horrible screams. Men were having legs and arms amputated without anesthetics of any kind. They had no anesthetics. Nothing to club down the demanding pain, as they had no food to fill hollow bellies, no shoes to protect the feet from the creeping winter.

But they would fight on, fight until the ammunition was gone until they hadn't the strength to pull a trigger. They would fight because they were fighting for their country—the Confederacy which was falling but would not go down without a last great roar, a great savage snarling battle cry, a striking out to let the men from the north, those who would be masters of the continent know that they might have the machinery, the mills, the numbers—but the South had the men!

"The colonel would like to see you, sir."

Morgan rose stiffly and buttoned up his tunic, dusting off the best way he could. Then he followed the corporal to the tent occupied by Colonel Fainer.

There were a half dozen strange horses ground-hitched nearby. An enlisted man stood watch over the horses. Distantly cannon fire echoed as the Union army advanced, eternally advanced, devouring the South.

Morgan knocked on the tent frame and was summoned. A dozen officers sat around the makeshift table inside Fainer's tent. The colonel himself rose to perform the introductions although Shelter knew most of them. Twyner, Plum up from Quartermaster, Major Swift from the Second Carolina. The man Morgan didn't know stood in the corner of the test smoking a cigar, the smoke rising in lazy wreathes. A stray beam of sunlight touched the star on his epaulet and Shelter frowned.

"Sit down, Shell," Colonel Fainer said warmly. "No need to stand on ceremony here." Which was an odd thing for Fainer to say. He was a good man, a good friend, but he was all military and he wouldn't tell a field-commission captain to sit while a general officer stood. It failed to touch off alarms in Morgan's brain, however; he simply sat, perching on an upturned barrel.

"Shelter Morgan?" the voice from the shadows asked.

"Yes, sir."

"I understand you know the area around Lookout Mountain."

"I know it as well as most, sir. I'm a Tennessee boy."

"Do you think you could get through the Yankee lines and get to Lookout, Captain Morgan?" the general asked suddenly. Shelter almost laughed, but there was no humor in the general's voice.

"It would be a dead toss-up, sir. Maybe. With a small force. It would have to be guerilla work. Civilian clothes, travelling at night mostly, keeping to the ridges . . . maybe."

"I have to know, Morgan. It's important."

Why in hell was everyone looking at him? Shell let his eyes take it in. Officers watching him anxiously. It was big whatever it was. He answered the general.

"It can be done, sir, yes."

"And you can do it."

"I can do it."

Colonel Fainer spoke up: "I don't have an officer more trustworthy than Shelter Morgan, sir. I don't have a man more qualified for this job. He was born in Pikeville, Tennessee—that's only a stone's throw from Lookout Mountain."

"Yes, Fainer, I'm aware of that." The general stepped into the light. His hair was silver, neatly barbered. His eyes were green, piercing. "We don't have much time, do we, to make a second choice?" He paused and puffed at his cigar again. "All right. Morgan, you're our man."

Colonel Fainer seemed to relax. He nodded at Morgan as if to congratulate him. Morgan didn't know what he was being congratulated for. The general told him.

"I was at Chickamauga, Morgan. It was a terrible defeat. We botched it. We were outgunned and outmanned, but we botched it, and damn us for that. The Union army just crushed our forces. We ran—they called it a tactical retreat, but it was a damned quick retreat. Supplies, valuable supplies were left behind near Lookout Mountain."

"What sort of supplies, sir?"

The general's eyes narrowed. "Negotiable supplies, sir." He came to within a pace of Morgan, those eyes narrowing still more. "It was gold, Captain Morgan. Gold which the South desperately needs. Gold to purchase ammunition, clothing, shoes, medical supplies —" as if to punctuate that remark a horrible cry of pain sounded from across the camp, from the medical tent where a man was being cut open with a knife, perhaps chopped at with a bone saw while four or five others held him down, held him down until the terrible waves of pain bludgeoned him into unconsciousness.

"Gold, sir," the general went on. "In the amount of a quarter of a million dollars."

"A quarter . . ."

"Have you any idea how much morphine, how many pairs of shoes and socks, how many bullets can be purchased with that money, Morgan? The British blockade runners are ready and willing to supply us."

Colonel Fainer spoke up again. "Shelter, if we can hold out another year, if we can make the Yankess eat fire and death long enough to negotiate a decent peace, a lot of pain will be saved the South. As it is now they will slaughter us. They will destroy us. We will be made to bow down to Washington and there will never again be a free baby born in Dixie. There will not be a home for any of us to go to—we will be branded outlaws, disenfranchised, our land sold from under us. Our women are going to be given over to the Yankees—that's the price of an unjust peace. If we can hold out through the winter, hold on one more year, maybe we can wring some concessions from Lincoln, Lincoln who only wants to crush us no matter what he says."

Across the camp the cry of pain sounded again and then broke off sharply. Death or merciful unconsciousness had taken the man. Morgan knew who it was—Herrick, one of his own men who had taken that northern patrol yesterday and come back with a shattered leg. Herrick who had looked to Morgan for help, who had clutched at his captain's sleeve, eyes begging for relief, for merciful death . . . well, maybe he had gotten his wish.

"Captain?"

Shelter was far away, but he came back quickly and he nodded. "I'll go, sir. Give me my own men, handpicked men, men I can trust, and we'll do that job for you."

And they did. They started out at night, the five of them, in civilian clothes, riding the high ridges, the deep dells. The gold was where the general had said it would be and they had pulled it out from under the noses of the Yankees. They had lost a man on the way back. Needlessly lost him, but with Shelter at their head they had recrossed the lines four days later the horses they led carrying a heavy burden—two hundred and fifty thousand dollars in gold.

The courier had cut them off before they reached Fainer's headquarters. "Please, sir, if you will follow me—Colonel Fainer and General Custis are waiting."

And they were waiting in the clearing on the ridge, the fire-blackened oaks all around them, the wind shifting the ashes of war as the horses stamped their feet and tossed their heads uneasily.

The colonel was there, General Custis sitting a white horse. With them were dozens of men. Some Shelter knew—mostly officers from Fainer's staff, a few enlisted men: senior NCOs, some Shell had never seen. They shared something in common. None of them wore the Confederate gray. They were in civilian clothes; they were armed and menacing.

"What the hell is this?" Shelter Morgan asked.

"Shell, you know what it is," Fainer said.

"Do I?" Shell glanced at the men beside him, Big Jeb Thornton, dark, dangerous Welton Williams, little Dink. Men who had ridden through hell with him on this mission and looked to be set up for another fast ride straight into fiery Hades.

"The war is over, Shell. The surrender hasn't been signed, but it's over. Everyone knows that we've gotten our butts kicked good and proper."

"All right—we've lost. So what? We've still got people fighting. We've still got people bleeding and suffering."

"There's not a lot that can be done for them, Shell," Fainer said almost mildly.

"Damnit, Morgan!" General Custis bellowed. "You can't be such a fool."

"A fool." Shelter mulled over that. Maybe he was. A fighter of lost causes, a believer in right and wrong, a man to whom honor meant something. He had made a promise to those who needed him, and that promise was going to be kept, the hell with the rest of the world! A fool, yes, he supposed so. Maybe you have to be a little bit of a fool to keep your manhood intact.

Shell glanced at those who sided him, the men who had been through four years of war with him. They knew. They knew and they stood with Morgan. It wasn't going to be enough, the four of them. Sitting their horses in the clearing were the others, the officers and NCOs the men had trusted, the leaders the fighting men would have followed into the flames of battle. Men who had turned their backs on the soldiers in their command and on the cause they fought for.

They couldn't ride out of that clearing and leave a witness to treachery alive.

"Well?" It was Custis again. "There's plenty for all of us, Morgan. There's no sense in making yourself a martyr. The war is done, we're done. They owe us something, don't they, for these years of combat and deprivation?"

"They didn't promise us anything, sir, but a soldier's pay, and we agreed to that."

"Shell, please . . ." Colonel Fainer said, and there was something approaching pain in his voice. Morgan just stared at him, stared at Fainer and the general, at the others who had thrown their lot in with these men. Officers Shelter had fought with, lived with, eaten with, shared dreams with. He looked at them slowly, one by one, etching their faces in memory. There were one or two whose names he did not know; one or two whose faces he could not see. That didn't matter—they were marked from that moment on.

Shell sat watching, seeing the hands of one man beyond Fainer's shoulder, seeing the hat which was tugged low in rudimentary disguise. He could see the silver mounted gunbelt the man wore, the silver spurs, but not his face.

He was looking at that and then he was looking into the hail of gunfire, the flames erupting from the muzzles of the gold-hunters, the frenzied eyes of the desperate men.

2.

Who fired first Shelter never knew. He only knew that the dogs of war had been cut loose again and he was in their path.

Sergeant Jeb Thornton was at Shell's side and Shell saw him hit, saw his throat torn away, saw the horse he rode rear up and dance away. Simultaneously Shell's own hand had filled with his handgun and he had fired nearly point blank into the face of a would-be killer.

Welton Williams was on Shelter's other hand, a cool, dark-eyed savage man who could hit what he aimed at with either hand. He was good, was Welton, but he couldn't stand up before two dozen strong men and trade lead with them. The bullets nearly cut him in half as the ambushers' guns spoke and Williams went down, his own horse trampling over him, crushing bone and muscle.

And then they were running. Dink and Morgan.

The Dink had lost his spectacles somewhere. He could only cling to the neck of his war horse, cling to it and then slowly slide to the cold earth as the seeking bullets from behind pursued them.

And then there was only Morgan left, Captain Shelter Morgan, CSA, running north, running hard as those he trusted tried to butcher him—and then, in the arms of those he hated, he found safety.

He ran smack into that Yankee patrol, too weak to fight, too weary to run, and he was arrested on the spot. Arrested as a spy and sentenced to prison in that Maryland fortress where more hundreds died, where more thousands were brutalized.

He didn't forget. Not for a moment in all of the seven years he spent in prison. He didn't forget them, and he made his vows. He promised himself and the cold gray walls of his cell that he would find them, every last one, and finish them.

"And that is what brought you to Hogan?" Lola asked. She was studying him intently, her fingers working steadily on his growing erection. She sat on the bed facing him, those great and wonderful breasts lifting and falling slowly, riveting Shell's attention.

"That's it," Morgan answered. Her hands were on his shaft and now his fingers slipped between her legs as they sat, knees touching. He spread her slowly and gently stroked the stiffening tab of flesh there as she shuddered and wrapped both hands firmly around him, leaning forward to meet him in one long kiss.

"Which one is it?" she asked. Lola had heard the story and now she was interested in it, wanting to know all there was about this strange bearded, blue-eyed man.

"His name was Kyle Cornelius—at least that's the name he enlisted under. I don't like the sound of the name and I haven't had a damn bit of luck finding out anything about him. It makes me think the name was an alias—no one cared a damn what your name was in those times if you were willing to put your hands around a gun and fire."

"I'm willing to put my hands around your gun and watch you fire," she said, earning herself another kiss.

"Anyway—take it easy there, woman—anyway, Cornelius like all the rest of them came West."

"Why is that?" Lola asked.

"Why? The law is small in numbers and far between. Out here no one asks what your name is, where you've been, where you're going."

"If you didn't even know this Kyle Cornelius, how do you know his name and where he is?"

"People talk to me, Lola. A lot of people. Every poor suffering Johnny Reb who dragged his ass around through the mud and snow that last winter, needing clothing and blankets and shoes. They knew about the gold, knew that their officers had betrayed them. Yes, they talked. They want them . . ."

"Dead," Lola said, bending her head so that her hair fell across Shell's lap. Her kisses were soft and searching.

"Caught," Shell amended. He had never set out to kill any of them in cold blood, although that was what they needed. But the majority of them had taken up bloody or at least illegal trades in the West. Once that easy money got into a man's blood, he was a goner it seemed. Some of those Shell had found had been jailed, a few legally hung. There had been a suicide and a score or more of those who had decided they just had to brace Shelter Morgan. Those were the dead ones. Those were the ones who had paid the price they owed.

"Someone told you about Kyle Cornelius."

"Someone told me. I mentioned something I'd seen.

A faceless man with a silver mounted pistol. It was a man in Los Angeles. His name's not important, but he had been in the Sixth Georgia and he had known a man—a man named Kyle Cornleius—who wore a fancy Colt Navy revolver. I went looking into Cornelius's past and came up a blank. He had enlisted out of Waycross, Georgia, up and bought a commission six months later. Won or purchased promotion to captain later that year, been assigned to the staff of General Custis—then nothing. Lost, assumed killed."

"He wasn't killed."

"I don't think so. I think he was running by then, his saddlebags filled with gold."

"Why did you come to Colorado though?" Lola was inching nearer now, trying her best to fit them together as they sat facing each other on the bed, and Lola's best was very good. Shell was losing the thread of the story.

"The man in Los Angeles—he has a brother out here, a brother who ran into a man with a silver mounted Colt. There was trouble about it, enough trouble to make it newsworthy and so he wrote home."

Lola's legs had gone out wide around Shell's waist. Now she inched forward, those amazing breasts flattening against Shell's chest as she slid onto him and clung to him, her breath warm and damp in his ear.

"Please," she said, "a little more forward, a little to the left—oh, Jesus, that's good, Morgan, very good!"

It was indeed. She seemed to have forgotten the topic of conversation. So had Shell, temporarily. He was more interested in the driving heat of her body, the lift and presss of the soft weight of her breasts, the damp intensity of her crotch, devouring and needful. He held her to him, holding her head with one hand, his other clenched on her amazingly strong haunch, feeling the slow pulsing of muscle there, the flex and release of tension as she thrust herself against him, becoming an engine of want which pressed and gobbled and absorbed, and was lubricated to overflowing before, satisfied, it purred to an aching halt, leaving a soft, intent glow behind.

Shelter Morgan rose and walked to the window to stand naked staring out at what there was of Hogan, Colorado, at the far spruce covered hills, the rain clouds drifting low across them, cutting off their heads, shading the valley to deep green. Silver rills raced off the flanks of the hills, forming delicate tracery against the grass. It would rain again, keep on raining. The storm had settled in.

Shelter looked back toward the bed. Lola had gone but her memory lingered, and a fine memory it was. She was a lot of woman, strong, earthy, giving, happy.

Shelter walked to the bureau where the kerosene lamp stood, lifted the chimney and lit the wick, watching the blue flame spread evenly from one corner across the length of the woven wick.

When he had the wick turned down properly he sat down on the single wooden chair the room had to offer. He sat there, watching the drops of metallic gray rain dribble down the pane of glass, hearing the wind whistle and challenge.

Then with a sigh, Shelter slowly began to dress. He reviewed the conversation he had had with Daltry Logan in Los Angeles.

"How do you know it's Kyle Cornelius, Logan?"

The little man finished his whisky, looked to Shelter who nodded assent, and ordered another from the harried barkeep in the busy saloon on Winslow Street. When Logan had that one firmly in his fist, he replied.

"My brother, Sailor Logan, has him a place in Hogan, Colorado. That's . . ."

"I know where Hogan is," Shell said. It was another

mining town pasted to the Rockies, sucking at the veins of silver and gold which riddled the ancient rock. It was another place Shelter had passed through, searching . . .

"In Hogan, Colorado." Logan said again, finishing his whisky in one gagging gulp. "Smooth, ain't it?" he said, casting one bitter glance at the bartender. "Anyway—they have been having themselves a hell of a time out there lately. Reason I know is Sailor asked me would I come out and stand behind a gun for him. Answer to that is 'no', of course. Brother or none—I spent four and a half years standing behind a gun, Captain Morgan. Enough's enough. A man can only stretch his luck so far." He looked beseechingly at Morgan again, received another nod of acquiescence and ordered another whisky.

"Thought it wasn't good enough for you," the bartender said sarcastically. "A connoisseur like you."

"Screw you. Pour it," Logan said. The bartender did so, slopping an ounce or two on the bar. When he walked away Shell tried to get back to the point.

"Your brother saw Cornelius. How does he know that it was Kyle Cornelius?"

"Well, he don't, you see. Me, once he wrote me the description, well I knew who it was. I was two years under Cornelius in the Alabama regulars. Two years, and what a bastard he was." Logan shook his head and tossed down his drink. When he asked again, Shell wagged his head negatively. At this rate by the time Logan decided to answer his questions, he wouldn't be able to.

"Your brother described him."

"Not exactly. Said they were having trouble with nightriders. Let me back away a bit and explain about that."

Shelter let him take the roundabout way. There was

no hurrying Daltry Logan on this night.

"When my brother first drove him some Texas cattle up to Hogan there weren't a dozen spreads in the territory—this was way back, you understand. Before the war. Well Sailor was doin' all right up there, a little yes and a little no if you understand me," Shelter nodded, "when some fellah hit gold in the area—Big Dome, Sailor calls it. Right away I guess about half a million more fellahs with picks come in and start pounding away at the ground, going off every which way like madmen, figuring on putting in a day's work and going home rich."

"They always do, but ninety-nine times out of a hundred it's the big operators that roll on and the little ones that get rolled over. It takes more than a pick and shovel to make that dirt pay."

"Sure, well you won't see me chasin' any gold strike though I've got a cousin . . . well, anyway," he said, noticing the annoyance on Shell's face. "First thing Sailor knows he's knee-deep in prospectors and that's a little yes and a little no too. They want to crawl over his land, maybe dig up his house to look for gold. Everywhere, he says, like swarmin' locusts. In his timber, sleepin' in his barn come winter, eatin' his beef, leavin' half a dead steer."

"I get the picture."

"Do ya? Say," Daltry Logan said, leaning toward Shell, "am I makin' this story too long?"

"Just get on a little, will you?"

"Sure, Captain. I forgot you ain't interested in family, just in Kyle Cornelius. I was saying that he got some bad, some good out of this gold rush, my brother Sailor Logan. They crawled all over his land and destroyed a lot of property—contrary wise, beef cattle suddenly became worth more than their weight in gold. Miners've got to eat, don't they? Well there was suddenly about half a million people standing around goin' hungry. Wasn't enough game in the territory to feed 'em if they knew how to hunt and wanted to spare the time from their diggin's. And they didn't."

"Your brother made a packet."

"He did that, sir. Not that it was worth the aggravation—that's what Sailor wrote, it wasn't worth the damned aggravation, but he's got the two youngsters, you see, and he wanted to put something by for them. Besides, if he didn't sell, they'd take. It was that way."

"Kyle Cornelius?" Shelter prompted.

"Okay. I'm gettin' there, Captain Morgan. A little cool tonight, ain't it?"

Shelter lifted a finger and the bartender came their way, refilling the glass on the counter in front of Daltry Logan.

"Now, next thing that happens is," Daltry began after finishing the drink, "other folks get the idea that beef is worth money. It's as good as gold, better than gold maybe. Easier to get at."

"Rustling."

"Rustling, yes," Daltry said. "By now there's a dozen small ranchers in the area, and all of them are getting hit regular. A tough bunch has moved in from somewhere, looking for the easy pickings and they figure they've got it. There's no army for five hundred miles and the only law they got is what the mine bosses can hire."

"The mines are getting hit too?"

"Sure. There night riders aren't above taking cash if they can locate it. They're out to empty everyone's pockets, you see."

"Just a regular outlaw gang."

"Not quite, no sir. What they've got is a reputation for being on the side of the poor, you see, on the side of the little man. Why—someone was thinking when he laid that course. No one ever sees the night riders when they ride past a camp, see. And in the morning, why they find a sack of dust or some gold money there and they go, 'Damn me, those night riders are fine fellahs.' I guess, according to Sailor, that they've spread the idea that they're fighting the war still, and . . ."

"They're what?"

"Fighting the war, captain. You know and I know that most everyone out West right now is from the South. The Yankees, why they went home after the war, didn't they? Us—where the hell did we have to go after they gave our land to the carpetbaggers and our women to the scalawags? West, the young and the able went west, those that didn't stay South to be locked up for goin' against the Official Policy of the United States Government, that is not letting themselves be run over by everyone who voted right or promised to vote right."

Daltry Logan shook his head unhappily, mulling over some personal injury, no doubt.

"Kyle Cornelius."

"Kyle Cornelius, yes. Well, these night riders who want everyone to think they're Southern rebels and a friend of the downtrodden, as it were, they got a man with them who wears a silver mounted Colt . . ."

"I've seen a dozen of them, Daltry," Shelter commented, though his heart had begun to pound a little. "Kyle Cornelius isn't the only man to ever wear a fancy gun."

"No, I guess he ain't, but these night riders one evening they came up to my brother's ranch which is the Double O, all wearin' masks and all, all threatenin'. Sailor went out onto the porch in his nightshirt, his little girl and his son inside at the windows, shotguns at the ready.

" 'Get off this land, you damned Yankee,' the leader of these night riders shouts, and my brother he stands up straight and tells 'em, 'Why, you cowardly hounds, why don't you go down South and fight if you got the hearts to fight the damned Yankess and their lackeys? Me, I'm up out of Tuscaloosa, and if any damned one of you calls that North, you can swing down and come up on this porch and prove it to me with a knife or gun or bare hands!' "

"Your brother's got some fire in him," Shell commented.

"Yes, he does. Sailor's been around half the world on sailing vessels, seen a lot I reckon in them foreign ports. He knows his way. He wasn't going to back down to no scum like these night riders.

"Their leader, now, he ups and says, 'You call yourself a Confederate—but you did not fight for the South, did you, Sailor Logan?'

" 'Why, damn you,' my brother answers, 'How the hell could I fight for the South away out here in Colorado? But I had four cousins that fought, three that died. An uncle that was killed at Manassas and a brother who was wounded at Sharpsburg.' . . . That being me," Daltry Logan said. "Got me through the thigh, high up. Come within an inch of the big artery, would have killed me dead there. Nicked off the hipbone. Pains me when it's cold weather, but didn't keep me out of the fighting for more'n four weeks. I was detached then to Cornelius's regiment—hell everyone was getting shifted around those days like cards being shuffled. You lagged you got left behind and hooked up with the next outfit that rambled past . . . well, you know all that."

"Yes. What did this night rider say to Sailor next?"

"What did he say? Well, sir, that was when he let it drop. 'Your brother a soldier! Why Daltry Logan was nothin' but a . . .' And that was it. He must've known he'd gone too far.

"Sailor told 'em to get off, that he was as Gray as any of 'em, more than most. He told 'em that and then told 'em there were two scatterguns peeking at them through the windows, and one or the other argument got through to them," Daltry said, chuckling dryly. "But he's still having trouble with them. Not as bad as as some, but enough. They kill, do the night riders, if they don't like your accent or the size of your purse."

"You figure, do you, that the man doing the talking that night was Kyle Cornelius?"

"How do you figure it, sir?" Daltry asked with a heavy, slow wink. "Who the hell would know me? Have to be someone I had met in the war. Someone who didn't like me a bit. Maybe someone who thought I was slackin' when I was recuperating from that leg wound. But this man also had to wear a silver-mounted gun, and Captain Morgan, there's only one man who fits all of them circumstances. So—do I *know* it was Kyle Cornelius? No, I reckon not. But you name me a more likely man."

"I can't do that, Daltry. No, sir," Shelter said, throwing down another silver dollar to refill Logan's glass. "I've got the same inclination you have—it's Kyle Cornelius or we've got a hell of a coincidence."

"Then you'll be going up to Colorado, sir?"

"Oh, yes, Daltry. I'll be riding that way."

Morgan didn't say anymore. He didn't have to. The tall man tugged his hat down and walked toward the saloon door and Daltry Logan watched him go, knowing that there was going to be killing at the end of Morgan's trail. Just then Daltry was glad of one thing—he hadn't been born with the name Kyle Cornelius. Because Cornelius, if he was in Hogan, Colorado, was already a dead man.

"Lou—fill me up again," Daltry Logan said. Then he took up a comfortable slouching position against the bar and prepared for a long hard night.

3.

Shelter Morgan pulled on his boots and tucked his shirt into his pants. Outside it was growing dark and the rain had begun to fall steadily. The main street of Hogan, Colorado was a wash of mud. Now and then a rider or a wagon would splash down the street, but the town itself was strangely silent, the rain muffling the noise emanating from the busy saloons.

Shell took his gunbelt from the bedpost and belted it on, checking the loads quickly. He knew Lola hadn't tampered with the gun, couldn't have—yet there had once been a woman he had trusted who had emptied his gun while he slept . . . may she rest in her hell.

Morgan snatched up his dark rain slicker and went out of the room.

One of the problems he had with this one was that he didn't know what Kyle Cornelius looked like. He knew the name, knew he had been attached to General Custis, knew he had been there on that bloody day, but what he looked like—no.

Daltry knew him well enough by sight, but Daltry was on a long downhill run into a whiskey barrel. Daltry could tell him that Cornelius was of medium height, dark haired, average weight, and that was it. No amount of questioning had pried any further details from the ex-soldier. His eyes? Brown or dark. Possibly blue if you pushed it. Really he hadn't noticed. But then men don't notice other men's eyes, that's all there is to that. Nose broken, narrow, wide? Kinda average, Daltry thought.

And on it went. An attempt at having Daltry draw Kyle Cornelius revealed nothing but the fact that Logan had the skills of a six month old child with a pencil . . .

"Going out, sir?" the desk clerk asked too cheerfully. Morgan could have made a clever reply or two, but he didn't. Where did the man think he was going if not out in a rain coat?

"I'm trying to look up an old friend," Shelter said. "Did you even hear the name Kyle Cornelius?"

"Sir?" the clerk looked completely blank.

"Kyle Cornleius."

"No, sir. And it's an unusual enough name, I'm sure I would have recalled it."

"Yeah. Thanks anyway." There was a dull little glimmer in the man's eyes, or there seemed to be. After a while, after years on the trail, you got a little odd, Morgan thought. Trust—why trust was something you placed in your gun hand or in your shooting eye, your reflexes, a length of finely honed steel. It wasn't to be given to human beings.

He went out into the rain to stand beneath the awning of the hotel, looking up and down the street. A wagon came slewing down the street, the teamster who drove it standing in the box shouting curses at his horses, curses that couldn't be heard above the driving rain.

Shelter turned uptown, walking slowly, his hand inside his slicker, resting on the butt of his Colt in a wholly natural way. You didn't trust anyone.

Across the street a dry goods store was open. Morgan saw no customers on this rainy night, just a balding clerk reading a newspaper across the counter.

The newspaper office was closed. They said it had been closed for months. No one in Hogan had had the time to read. There was gold to be had and that was all that mattered.

Too bad. Shelter had hoped to look through the back issues of the paper and get some idea of what was going on in Hogan. The only thing everyone seemed to agree upon was that anarchy was a way of life. The gun was law and the most guns won the election, irregular as they were.

The night riders had the most guns.

Morgan was walking slow, the rain was a steady wash of wind and water out of the north, smothering the town. It was dark and the streets deserted.

And there was someone walking in his footprints.

He knew that as he knew the rain was falling, the wind blowing—his senses told him. Not the workings of logic, but the softer senses. He *felt* the man back there.

He felt him and when he stopped to look across the street at the Sundown Saloon, he glanced in back of him and saw the flitting shadow dart into the muddy alleyway.

A slow smile curved Shelter's lips. There was just no reason at all for anyone to follow him—unless he was on the right track. Unless Kyle Cornelius was in Hogan and he knew. Knew that he had to kill Morgan or be killed.

It was, Shelter thought, going to be very easy after all.

He turned away from the main street and started off down a side road, taking his shadow with him. A closed and locked blacksmith's shop stood to the right, a warehouse of some kind to the left. Farther on was a farrier and a brick manufacturing plant. Morgan had seen two brick buildings in Hogan and one brick house on the outskirts. Optimists everywhere. If the town lasted one day longer than the ore in the hills, Shelter would be surprised.

He swung to his right, entering the narrow passageway between the smith's and the farrier's.

Lightning flickered in the distance. Thunder rolled down the mountain slopes beyond Hogan. Shelter Morgan inched down the alleyway, his back to the blacksmith's shop, his Colt held high beside his ear. Rain trickled from his hat brim, glistened on his black slicker.

The man appeared at the head of the alley and there was enough light for Morgan to see that he had a long gun in his fists. A shotgun or a rifle. A shotgun if he was good. He seemed to hesitate at the head of the alley. Morgan smiled thinly. He didn't know Morgan was in the alley. He thought so, but he was guessing. It was tough on the dark night.

The stalking man remained fixed, his silhouette momentarily stark against the background of flickering yellow lightning.

"You're gone, my friend," Shell thought. Easy as a kid's puzzle. One, two, three. No more stalking man.

That was what Morgan thought one moment. The next he discovered he was caught in a death trap.

He heard the scuffling noise at the other end of the alley. Ahead of him now. A quiet scraping. Boot leather on gravel and he froze, pressing himself to the wooden wall of the blacksmith's.

"Hal?" The voice was a whisper which barely carried to Shell. There was no answer. After a minute though a quiet whistle came from behind and above.

On the roof!

How the hell had they gotten there? He supposed there were any number of ways. How didn't matter now. Getting out did.

Shell looked right and then left. The rain slanted down heavily, silver ribbons falling earthward. He found the shuttered alley window and shoved against it with his hand. No luck. He tried his shoulder with the same results.

From the front of the alley someone started walking toward him, hearing the noise no doubt. Another whistle. Either above or at the end of the alley. The rain and wind confused the senses.

Shelter took a long step back and hurled himself at the shuttered window. The shutters creaked and snapped on their hinges and Shelter was up and into the musty building. Behind him a voice shouted.

"There he is!"

But he wasn't there any more and the shotgun which cut loose behind him, smearing the wet walls of the alley with blinding reddish-yellow light, hit nothing.

"God damn you, you idiot!" the man at the foot of the alley bellowed. "You nearly got me."

Morgan heard that through the wall, then the sound of other rushing footsteps.

A man peered in the window. "I think he's in here," he hissed, and Shelter shot him.

The .44 angled up, chipped a long jagged splinter from the lintel of the blacksmith's window and drove into the man-hunter's throat, removing the middle of his chin, the back of his head.

"Jesus!" someone yelled. There was another loud

exclamation and then abrupt silence as they figured out their turns could be next.

Shelter crossed the smith's barn, listening, watching front and back doors. They had someone on the roof as well, maybe more than one man, and there was a good chance there was a loft and trap door somewhere if the building ran true to type.

There wasn't much to be cheered about; Morgan was trapped. They couldn't fire the place in this weather, and that was about all he could think of that was good about the situation.

He crept toward the front door, crouched low behind the partitions which divided the stalls where horses and wagons, buckboards were kept waiting for their owners or the smith's convenience. Farm equipment of various types lay around the barn, a large harrow dead in the middle of the room, a thresher leaning against the far wall, its frame cracked, awaiting the blacksmith's welding talents.

The front door opened and two men appeared there, the wind whipping their rain slickers around their knees. One of them yelled out.

"Haraahgh," and cut loose with a rifle. The bullets sang off wagon hubs, the harrow, the steel strapping on the back door of the barn. Shelter hit the ground and rolled away into the darkness which was nearly total.

That didn't stop the two gunnies from trying to kill him. They couldn't see him, but they seemed to think their bullets had eyes. They emptied the magazines of their rifles into the barn, throwing splinters everywhere. The horses shrilled their panicked objections.

Shelter Morgan kept low behind the partition where the smith had his bellows and anvil. He crept toward the door. Looking between the planks in the partition he could see two pairs of legs. They had unlimbered their sixguns and were shooting at something unseen.

Morgan propped up, sighted his Colt carefully and squeezed off, blowing one of them away to collide with the other and knock him down.

The dead man was slowly rolled aside. Shell could hear the panting as the second killer tried to crawl out from underneath.

"Hold it there if you want to live, my friend," Morgan said quietly.

He didn't want to live. He brought his Colt around and Morgan's pistol bucked twice in his hand, gouting red-orange flame. The hot lead slammed into the badman's chest, twisting him around, driving him to the ground to lie there unmoving, silent. He was quite dead.

The barn door flapped in the wind, but Shelter didn't try for it just yet. He held his position, believing always that patience was worth a moment's heroics.

In ten minutes another head poked in the door. Whether he saw Shell in that light or not, this one cut loose with a scattergun and it was damned close, too close as Morgan hit the the straw-littered floor of the shop.

He lay there panting, the Colt warm in his hand. They had chosen a good night for it, the bastards. No one would come running to see what was happening on this night. The sounds of the storm covered all else. A charge of dynamite going off in the middle of Main Street wouldn't have been heard.

The man with the scattergun had withdrawn. Shell could see nothing of him but one corner of his slicker whipping back and forth in the wind, the toe of one boot. He was waiting. Waiting for what?

For the others to get into position, no doubt. Shell glanced up. Was that a footstep on the roof? He knew there was someone up there. Was he making his move?

Hell, yes he was. If Morgan had been running this

operation he'd have his man come down behind the quarry too. He eased back, eyes trying to probe the darkness, desperately trying to make out the lay of the building.

Distant lightning flickered dully, thunder pealing on its heels and Shell smiled crookedly. The lightning had shown him all he wanted.

In the back of the building was a loft, a sort of half-ceiling used for tools and hay. Above the loft, cut into the back wall was a narrow window where a boom could be mounted. There, then. It was there that the man on the roof would come down.

Shell eased toward the back wall, his boots moving softly over the hay and mulch scattered about the earthen floor. A horse nickered as Shell passed it and he rested his hand gently on the animal's shoulder, quieting it.

Something moved overhead. The boards creaked again and Shell moved to the back wall, looking up at the half-ceiling. Someone was definitely in the loft now. As he moved forward along the gallery dirt sifted down from between the planks, falling like gentle, telling rain. Shelter crouched, watching.

He glanced at the back door, wondering how many were out there. In front was the man with the scattergun—that was a bad risk no matter what kind of eye was behind it. He wasn't going to miss.

A little more dust sifted down and Shell smiled thinly, moving to the back door in three easy steps. He could see nothing for a long while, nothing but the rain lashing down, the cold steel-colored puddles on the bare gound outside the smith's barn. Then he picked up movement. One man, no two, behind a hay wagon. One lifted his arm in signal. All right then—three men at least; he had to be signalling to someone.

And no good exit from that yard that Morgan could

see. He frowned and moved back into the silence of the barn. They had him nailed down good and proper. It bothered him, bothered him badly. These men were quite serious, well-prepared, ready to pay the price. How the hell did Cornelius know? It had to be Cornelius, didn't it?

Well, it didn't have to be—there were a lot of men down Shelter's backtrail, a lot with a heavy grudge.

"I could have been talking to Cornelius here and not known it," Shell thought disgustedly. It was true. How many dark-haired, "average" men had he talked to? Men changed too. Look at old Joe Bass down in Jacumba—thin as a whip, dark haired, almost fleshless and when Morgan last saw him he weighed every bit of three hundred pounds, had snowy hair and enormous jowels . . . he was also dead when Morgan left Jacumba.

The feet in the loft moved again and Shell made his decision. He needed some confusion to accomplish what he wanted so he moved back along the stalls where the horses were kept, untying them, slapping them on the rump to get them out of the compartments. One of them nickered, tossing its head, Shell glanced up at the loft, half-expecting a shot to ring out. Nothing. They couldn't see him.

The front door was already open and now Shelter moved to the back door. He lifted the bar and slid it aside. Then he touched the bottom of the door frame with his boot toe and it swung silently open.

Morgan stood well back. Outside they would be alerted, ready to kill. A low whistle sounded. Shelter barely heard it as he moved through the knot of horses toward the ladder to the loft.

He paused, eyes bright in the shadows. His Colt was in his hand as he began climbing the vertical wooden ladder, using one hand. The rat was still up there.

Shelter heard him move, a faint whisper like a mouse scuttling across the floor of the loft. Shell swung to the inside of the ladder, climbing up the back of it, eyes alert, his thumb on the heavy curved hammer of the Colt.

He was three rungs from the top when the pistol was thrust down through the trap door. Three shots cracked in the night, flame stabbing at the darkness. The bullets would have hit him had he been climbing the ladder on the front side. As it was Shell had time to sight, to trigger off one round and watch as the screaming man tumbled past to land flat on his back against the floor.

The horses whinnied in fright and began to run as the shots were fired. They needed no help but Shelter gave them some, another round fired into the air, and the panic increased.

They split, half the herd going for the front door, the others for the back.

"The horses! Stop the damned horses. He'll be hanging onto one of them!"

Which was what Shelter wanted them to think—that he was making his escape in the cover of the horse herd. But he was nowhere near them. He had chosen the weak spot to break through and right or wrong he wasn't going to stop now.

Shelter swung up into the loft, crouched and steadied himself. But there was no sniping fire. He crossed the loft quickly, locating the trap door to the roof easily. The cold wind blew down through it and compared to the darkness of the loft, even the tumbling gray skies outside were bright.

Shelter went up and through, dropping the trap behind him. Then he waited on his haunches, looking along the roof of the smith's shop, seeing no one against the sky, no one waiting to cut him down.

From somewhere below the sounds of cursing, the

trampling of hoofs sounded, but all of that was distant now. Shelter crossed the roof, leaped the alley and rolled onto the tarpaper roof of the farrier's barn. Crossing that he found an outside ladder leading down to a second alley. There was no one below when Shelter reached the ground, no one at the head of the alley. He crossed the street, passed the brickworks and headed up the main street, whistling as he walked.

4.

Morning was bright, clear. The clouds above the mountains were white, floating placidly southward, casting moving cloud shadows on the grassy valleys. To the north the clouds bunched in angry gray covens; it would rain again.

Shelter's blue roan moved out at a brisk pace, glad to be free of the stable once again, to be stretching its long limbs, breathing in and blowing out the chill air. The horse sunk to its hocks at the crossings, but Morgan kept to the hills where he could.

There was no sense in giving a sniper the advantage.

The town had been in something of an uproar that morning. Shell, rolling from the bed had asked Lola about it.

"Somebody broke into the smith's barn and cut all the horses free. They thought it was kids at first, but they found Bob Beamer dead. Gunshot."

She turned toward him, looking very pretty outlined against the cool blue glass of the window pane.

"Who was Beamer?" Shell asked, rubbing his head.

"Just an idler. Bummed drinks at the Red Dog Saloon nights. Slept days, I suppose. I never saw him in the daytime . . . say, Morgan, you're awful interested in things."

"Am I?" Shell asked innocently.

"Yes, you are." Lola stood, hands on hips, her wrapper gaping open, peering at the tall man.

"Just curiosity."

"I bet. You're still looking for him aren't you?"

"For who?"

"Cornelius."

"You'd do best to forget that name, Lola," Morgan said quite seriously. "And to forget that I've got a name."

"Oh, hell, I'll do that right enough, Shell." She waved a hand at him and crossed to the bureau where she kept her packet of thin cigars. Lighting one she waved out the match. "I've been up and down the street, you know. I've learned to keep my mouth shut."

"Just a reminder, Lola. Don't take it personal." Shell rose and crossed the room toward his clothes. Lola watched him appreciatively.

"My God, what a man," she said. "Got a few fresh scratches on you, don't you?"

"Do I?"

"Morgan—I know every inch of that fabulous body of yours. They're new. As of last night."

"Fell out of bed, I guess." Shell yawned and pulled on his trousers.

"I guess," Lola laughed, puffing out a cloud of cigar smoke. "You'd better keep quiet about whatever went on last night. Folks are smoking mad about those horses being lost." Lola sat on the chair, crossing her long legs which the wrapper did little to cover.

"Shelter? What next?"

"What have you got in mind?"

"Don't clown. You're riding out aren't you?"

"I thought I might take a little look around the area. Who knows," he shrugged. "I might want to settle here."

"You'll settle all right. They'll bury you," Lola said with some anger. "If you keep poking around asking about those night riders, Morgan, they will bury you."

Shelter nodded. He was standing before the mirror, stroking his beard. "I think it's about time this thing goes, don't you?"

"How would I know—I never saw you without it. Maybe you don't even have a chin. You don't seem to have any ears," Lola said with disgust.

She got up, walked to the window again and stood looking down at the street. Dropping the cigar to the floor she toed it out and then walked to Morgan who was dressed but for his gunbelt.

"You're not going to make trouble, are you, Morgan?"

"Of course not." He kissed her. "Your ear tastes delicious this morning."

"Don't start that if you're planning on leaving—please." Lola leaned back and looked up at him. "You're going to go riding, aren't you?"

"That's right."

"Why?" Her hands dropped in exasperation. "Why, Morgan? What in hell's the matter with men! Here I am—take me, lay me down and screw me. Why in hell would any man rather go out and get himself shot to stew meat?"

There wasn't a good answer to that. Not one that Lola could understand anyway. But then Lola had never seen the boys with their feet amputated, those who hadn't gotten the shoes and the blankets Kyle Cornelius and the others were going to purchase for them. She hadn't seen that cold, horrible mass grave in Georgia where they lay—the boys of Alabama and Mississippi, of Texas and Georgia and Carolina, North and South, of Louisiana, Florida, Virginia and Arkansas and Tennessee. Dead, many of them from Yankee bullets, but some from the treachery of their own leaders.

You don't explain the sight of those graves on a cold windy day. You just live with it, and the rage burns for a long while, a very long while indeed.

The wind was brisk whistling down the long timber-covered slopes. Above the hills the purple-gray Rockies with a new dusting of snow marched away toward the south and north, their heads lost in the sky.

Shelter tugged up the collar of his coat and paused to pull his gloves on. He sat the blue roan looking for landmarks. The Logan ranch, the Double O, was another five miles on supposedly, in a high valley above the present range of hills.

The Logan ranch was his destination. If he could trust anyone at all in these hills, it was Sailor Logan, Daltry's brother. If anyone had a reason to dislike the night riders, it was Logan. And, if Daltry had told the story accurately, Sailor Logan was a tough nut. He had stood up to the night riders and backed them down.

There was one other benefit to visiting Logan. He had seen the man with the silver mounted Colt. He had seen him and spoke to him.

Was it Cornelius or not? Shelter still wasn't sure. He wanted to believe it was, but he was withholding judgment. No sense in getting himself excited about it. He had learned not to expect the trail he rode to be too easy.

The bay horse was just standing in the pines. Standing there and looking at Shelter Morgan. Its saddle was twisted around under its belly and it looked worn to a nub, gaunt and wary.

"Hold up." Shell slowed the roan and circled it, walking back through the trees toward the bay which backed away.

"Easy, boy. What's the matter? Lost your rider, didn't you?"

Shell swung down and walked to the bay which was wary still, but remained fixed in position. The animal seemed to need a human being, to want human company and leadership. Shell reached out and caught up the reins which had been trampled on as the horse ran. He patted the bay's neck and moved to the saddle.

There were dark streaks on the flanks of the bay, dark streaks on the saddle leather. Dry, crusted, deep maroon, it didn't take a lot of imagination to figure out what it was.

"Lost him good and proper, didn't you?" Shell said. He uncinched and let the saddle fall to the ground. There were some saddlebags on back, but there was nothing in them. Clean underwear, soap, some tinned beef.

"Where in hell is he?" Shell looked upslope and then down. It would take some tracking over this pine-needle covered earth. "The road most likely, unless he's a night rider."

The brand the bay wore was an oddball one, and X overlayed on a spiral. That was a new one on Morgan and he could only shrug. The bay was a strapping animal, well fed, well bred. It had a white blaze and a white stocking on the left front leg. It was a fine looking horse, too fine for a child, for a farmer, too big for a woman. That left outlaws and long travelling men. A long travelling man who had stopped travelling almighty short.

"Let's go," Shelter said. He led the bay back to where his roan stood with its ears pricked curiously. The two geldings were a little stand-offish, having no possible interest in one another.

Shelter rode down the mountain and then back up, following the little creek that ran there until he found hoofprints in the mud. Hoofprints belonging to the bay.

"That way," Shelter said, and he was frowning. He stroked his beard as he peered into the deep shadows of the pines. It wasn't the best of ways to ride, the timber was awfully thick for a horse.

"Well, then, there's a reason," Morgan said. But what it was he couldn't guess. A wounded night rider hiding in the timber? Why? Wouldn't his friends take care of him? From what Shell had been able to learn the night riders didn't have anyone to hide from anyway, no one to fear. They pretended to be a gang of Southern heroes, out to protect the small and the poor, and apparently they had gotten away with that routine. The locals wouldn't breathe a word about the night riders, not a bad word—Morgan knew, he had tried hard enough to pry something out of people.

"Christ!" Shell breathed. "Hold up." He slowed the roan and swung down again. There he was, tied to the trunk of the big pine, his plaid shirt soaked through with blood. The bay nickered and back away nervously.

"Easy boy," Shelter said. He had his gun in his hand now, and he looked around carefully, seeing nothing but the dark forest, the jays and the silver squirrels, the snowy clouds drifting past above the treetops.

Shell moved in nearer, seeing the hands bound tightly behind the back, the open mouth, the dark beard, the dark pool of blood saturating the ground.

There was something wrong, something. . . .

"Damn me," Shelter breathed. "Damn me for a Yankee!"

It should have struck him right away, but it hadn't. Maybe it was because of the beard. Shelter had never worn one for long and now he was. So was the dead man. That was only the beginning of the similarity.

The dead man had cold blue eyes, eyes which now looked vacantly out at the dark pines. He was a tall man, two inches over six feet easily, and he had dark hair, a narrow mouth, even nose, broad forehead—Shelter Morgan was looking at himself!

"If I had a brother, my friend, it would be you." Shell went a step forward and crouched down. The nearer he got the greater the resemblance. "Why?"

Why in hell had they killed this man? There was a chill crawling up Morgan's spine. "Because they took you for me?" Possible, it seemed very possible, but he didn't want to jump to conclusions.

He examined the man more closely. They had held him captive for a good long time. They had talked to him, taunted him perhaps. Small knife jabs along the ribcage, in the meat of the thighs indicated some sort of systematic torture.

Then, somewhere along the line, the man had just given it up. Bled to death.

"Dirty bastards," Morgan said softly. He could stand a lot, but he couldn't stand a torture-killer. Someone who liked to inflict pain, to watch another human being slowly expire.

Shell opened the man's shirt and it was only then that he saw the star, pinned to the inside of the shirt. The badge read United States Marshal. It hadn't done him a lot of good. The night riders had gotten him. Or Morgan assumed it was the night riders. It had to be, didn't it?

In another five minutes he was sure.

In an inside pocket he found the letter, the open warrant, the identification.

"J. T. Forsberg. United States Marshal, Denver office," Morgan read, shaking his head. He glanced over the identification and tucked it away in his own coat pocket. The letter was in a woman's hand.

> *"Dear Marshal,*
> *You do not know me but we've had a deal of trouble up here and it has become necessary for me to write to you. What has happened here in Hogan, Colorado, is that a gang of thugs has moved in and is making a mockery of law and order. We are being overrun by outlaws and there is no one to stand up to them, let alone for a woman's sake.*
>
> *We need help badly up here, sir, and so I am asking, please, send the law into Hogan, Colorado as I guess no one else has even thought to care if we have the law here or are all just butchered in our sleep.*
>
> *I am respectfully y'rs,*
> *Jean Waltham*
> *Sky Ridge Ranch*
> *Hogan, Colorado"*

The signature was childish scrawl. The ink had faded and run some from being in the weather. Shell shook his head and tucked the letter away too.

"Sorry, Jean Waltham, whoever you are, your marshall won't be coming."

There was a blank bench warrant in the marshal's pocket as well, meant to be filled out when the marshal discovered the identities of those he wanted to arrest. There was a blood stain on one corner of the warrant.

Morgan found a little hollow where he dumped the body of the lawman, scraping up pine needles and earth enough to cover him, rolling a few large rocks over the grave to keep the scavengers out. Then he stood there pondering the night riders, the marshal, and a lady named Jean Waltham.

"Damned fool thing to try," he said to himself. Then he opened his hand, looked at the badge he held there and pinned it on to his shirt front.

"I'll give it a try, partner," he told the dead man. "Maybe I'm out of my depth, but I'll try it."

Why he was going to try it he didn't know for sure, he didn't need the problem, that was certain. But he was going to try—he was after a band of men now, not a single night rider. He wanted not only Kyle Cornelius, but all of them. All of them who rode around this country bullying men like Sailor Logan, frightening women like this Jean Waltham, killing lawmen who dared to ride in to try putting a stop to their thieving, their brutality.

"I'll give it a try, marshal," Shelter said, and then he turned away, stroking his beard, looking thoughtfully toward the high peaks as the dark clouds from the north began to drift over again. It had been something to bury Marshal J.T. Forsberg. If the resemblance hadn't been so strong maybe it wouldn't have touched Shell at all—as it was, it was like burying himself, seeing his own eyes looking up into the cold gray skies, eyes which seemed to be asking a favor.

Retribution.

Last night Shelter had been surprised that they had come after him as they had, a half dozen strong, knowing what he looked like.

"Maybe," he thought, "they weren't looking for me at all. Maybe they were looking for J.T. Forsberg."

Then again, it could be that a man named Kyle Cornelius was trying to kill Captain Shelter Morgan, CSA when he killed Forsberg. One thing was certain—

someone was going to get a hell of a surprise when Morgan showed up wearing that badge.

The skies lowered as Shelter rode higher into the hills. He intended still to ride to the Double O and look up Sailor Logan, but that might have to wait. The clouds ducked their heads and began to rain, shutting out the landmarks as the wind swayed the deep ranks of pines. Wherever the Double O was Morgan wasn't going to find it except by accident.

The first steer he came upon lifted its head and shook water-glossed horns at him before returning to its fitful grazing. The brand on its flank was a "JW".

Jean Waltham? Maybe. Shell rode on through the narrow valley. The rain was coming down heavily now, stinging exposed flesh, birthing quick-running silver rills which wound across the bright green grass in the high meadows.

More cattle now, and the beginnings of a regularly used trail. And farther on the sign tacked to the old cedar tree. "Sky Ridge Ranch property. Keep out. We patrol armed."

Shell tugged down his hat and started up the trail. If they patrolled armed they didn't do a lot of it in weather like this. At least he hoped not.

He rode on through the pines which pressed against the trail. Lightning bridged across the gray skies leaving the scent of sulfur in the air. Thunder boomed uninterruptedly up the long canyons, so near and so heavy that it wasn't until the second shot that Shelter realized he had been tagged and that the thunder he heard was the report of the killing guns.

5.

Shelter flung himself from the stirrups. As he hit the ground rolling, his shoulder aflame with pain, the blue roan danced away, followed by the bay. A second shot thundered down the slopes, tearing a fist-sized chunk of bark from the pine beside Shell's head. He rolled to a stop, angrily yanked his Colt from its holster and started moving upslope, circling toward the sniper through the ground mist, the driving rain.

He hadn't paused to look at his shoulder wound. Either it wasn't terribly bad or shock was holding back the wash of pain that would soon follow. Either way he had to move now. Either way he wanted to stop the sniper cold in his tracks, cut him down before he could finish Shelter Morgan, finish him for good and all to lay in a cold unmarked grave next to his double.

The rifle upslope barked again, but the shot was far wide. Shell smiled grimly. The sniper had lost his target in the rain and fog.

Shell hadn't lost his. The report of the rifle was distinct now, near at hand, and he moved that way, climbing higher yet, wanting to be behind and above the rifleman.

He was a shadow drifting through the forest, a bearded stalking thing with a cold glint in his eyes, his teeth bared in a crooked grin. He moved through the trees like a whisper in the wind.

There. A patch of color against the grey-green of the day. Something red where nothing red belonged and Shelter began to stalk with slow patience, to move from tree to tree letting the wind rush cover his footsteps. The Colt was held before him, ready to speak its message of death.

One more step and then another and Morgan stepped into the clearing. His finger was already tensing on the trigger when he recognized the target for what it was.

"A damned woman," Shelter said in disgust and he lowered his weapon.

He lowered his, not willing to gun down a woman, but the fact that he was a man didn't stop the girl from turning and triggering off that Henry repeater. The bullet flew past Shell's head, clipped bark from an overhanging branch and sang off into the forest. Morgan dove to one side in a measured roll which brought him up behind a massive, pocked spruce tree.

Peering around the tree Shelter saw the girl take the rifle to her shoulder again, again squeeze the trigger. The hammer fell with a dull click. She had used her last round and the girl's great blue eyes went wide as she snatched at her bulky, man-sized coat's pockets for fresh cartridges.

Shelter was to her in four bounding strides. He grabbed the barrel of the Henry and twisted, tearing it from her hands. He threw it behind him angrily. The girl backed away, her eyes going wider yet, her mass of light brown curly hair blowing free in the wind.

She was most of five feet all, cute as a nubbin, she was also quite deadly. Shell's shoulder was leaking liquid fire at that moment.

"I ought to tie you to that tree and blister your fanny for you, woman. Damn you! What's the idea of shooting at me."

"Did I miss? I'm sorry if I missed," she spat back. She had her hands on her hips, her head thrust toward Morgan aggressively. "I meant to split your brisket open for you."

"Damn you, you little . . ."

"Don't cuss at me, mister. I don't take to it. Ain't fittin for a man to cuss a woman."

"But it's fittin to shoot a man?" Shelter was still advancing relentlessly, the woman still backing away, her index finger raised admonishingly. She waggled that finger at Shell.

"I'm not so sure you are a man. Your kind," she said. She backed roughly into a big pine and stood there, hands behind her back, holding onto it.

The rain slanted down from out of a gray sky. Distant thunder burbled and grumped over the hills. The pines were damp, their scent ripe in the cold air. And Shelter Morgan had himself a wildcat cornered.

"You don't have another gun on you, do you, woman? Some kind of little hideaway piece?"

"If I do it's none of your concern," the woman shot back, those eyes flashing and sparkling.

"Lady, I've got a hole in my shoulder. I don't know how bad it is. I haven't got the heart to look right now. But when I do look I don't want the person that put the first hole in my hide coming up and putting another one there. Yes, ma'am, it is my business. Take off your coat please."

"I will not!"

"Yes you will, and you'll do it now."

"What are you going to do, shoot me?" she taunted.

"Maybe. Maybe so." Shell tried to smile at this pint-sized she-devil. He tried but the pain in the shoulder made it difficult. It continued to remind him that however small she was, however much a girl, she had been intending to kill him and came near as damn to achieving it.

"Get that coat off," he growled.

"Then what?" she asked, only she was stuttering a little as she said it.

"Then I'm going to look for another gun. It's painless, won't take a second."

"You're going to *touch* me?"

"Lady, you've got nothing I haven't seen before."

"No, I suppose not—a man like you," she said disparagingly. Then martyr-like she shed the coat and stood there, arms raised.

It didn't take a second to find out that she wasn't carrying another gun. Shell patted down the pockets of the oversized pants she wore, turned her, checking the waistband and told her to put her coat back on. She hadn't anything any other woman didn't, but what she had was well-molded, very nice indeed . . . if you're thinking along those lines. Morgan wasn't.

He was thinking more along the lines of first aid. How he was going to get to that wasn't clear in his mind.

"I'm afraid I'm going to have to tie you up, at least loop your hands to a branch."

"You're what!"

"Please, don't give me any more trouble. I've got to see to this shoulder of mine." As he talked, Shell shed his own coat and tossed it aside. The girl gasped, put a hand to her lips and pointed, gurgling something.

She repeated it. "You're a lawman! You're the marshall I sent for!" The badge glittered dully on Shell's shirtfront.

"You're Jean Waltham."

"Yes, yes—how did I . . . ? I couldn't have known, could I?"

"You could have asked," Morgan replied. He had shed his shirt as well now. The cold air raked his body, numbing it. His shoulder was a point of heat and pain. It wasn't bad, but it wasn't good either. The bullet had lifted up a flap of flesh and hide and the blood seeped out unremittingly.

"I'm sorry, so sorry," the girl gasped.

"So am I, lady. It hurts like bloody hell—if that's not too strong a language for you."

"I'm sorry," she repeated. "Let me take care of it, please. You can't bandage that with one hand."

"All right." Morgan sighed. "You're right. I can't do much of a job here."

"Up at my cabin," she said. "This is no place to work. I've got hot water and bandaging."

"All right," Morgan said. It was beginning to rain much harder now. It drove down through the trees, stripping the loose pinecones from the branches, whipping the limbs of the trees around. The wind was cold and steady. Nothing sounded better just then than four walls and a fire. Shelter slipped his coat over his shoulder and swung up into the saddle.

"Can I get my rifle?" Jean Waltham asked.

"Go ahead—if you can find it." It was empty anyway. Shelter watched the girl search the underbrush and return with the Henry. He was sitting on his blue roan, holding the marshal's bay on a lead rope.

The girl glanced at him, held the rifle up sheepishly and then turned to walk upslope through the dark gray forest.

The cabin was half mile on, sitting small and squat among great wind-formed pines. Behind the house a rocky bluff rose. Below was a small meadow where cattle grazed and then a long escarpment, the land dropping off five hundred feet or so rapidly. On a clear day she would have been able to see miles in that direction, which if Shell hadn't gotten himself turned around, meant back toward Hogan itself.

Shell swung down heavily, keeping his eyes on Jean Waltham at all times. It's not that easy to forget that someone's shot you. It may have been an accident, very probably was. She may be cute as a bug and most friendly, but you remember still—This woman could have killed me.

She had the door open and Shell had loosened his cinches and tied the horses loosely to the hitchrail in front of the cabin. There were other tracks there the rain hadn't quite washed away. Three horses. Looking around casually, Morgan saw no sign of them.

"Come in, quickly," Jean said. The rain was hammering down and it seemed like a fine idea. Shell went up on the porch and through the door into the dark interior of the cozy cabin.

"Sit down, please. In the big chair."

Shelter walked to it, looking around the cabin. An Indian rug hung on the wall. There was a puncheon table and two chairs at it, a tiny kitchen beyond where a stone and sheet-iron stove sat. Then a hanging rug, a bedroom beyond that no doubt. A fireplace up against one wall, an old Kentucky long rifle hung above the stone hearth.

There was a fire banked in the fireplace and the girl squatted down, poking and prodding it to life. Shelter sat in the high backed leather and pole chair, watching the concentration on the girl's face, the light which flickered alive in her wide blue eyes as the fire came to life.

"I'll be with you in a minute. First I want to get some water starting to boil."

She walked to the kitchen, shedding the man-sized coat she wore, revealing again her pert figure wrapped up in a blue and black plaid cotton shirt. Shell watched the fire dance and crackle, watched the woman digging out a black iron pot.

She must have had water in the kitchen, for she didn't go out to a well, but walked to the fireplace lugging a big pot. Shell's shoulder was throbbing heavily, but his senses were alert despite the pain.

The three horses outside—recent visitors. Now he considered this: on entering the house he had been aware of woman-scents, of faint lavender and spice—but there had been another odor, faintly lingering, that of a cigar.

Now it was true Lola Allison smoked a thin cigar, but it couldn't have been that common around Hogan for the ladies to use them. Jean Waltham didn't look the type anyway. No, she had a man here, that was all there was to it . . . or a recent male visitor.

"Hold on now and I'll get this washed good and proper." Jean carefully peeled away the rough bandage Shell had knotted around his shoulder, an old scarf once blue, now deep maroon with blood. With two fingers she tossed that aside and, pursing her lips, she examined the bullet hole.

The fire was warm. Outside the rain pattered down. The woman was close against him, her breasts pressing against his shoulder as she moved, her breath warm and intent as she washed the wound.

"It won't stop bleeding, darnit," she muttered. "I'm going to have to sew this up."

"Go ahead."

"It'll hurt."

"I thought it might," Morgan said dryly.

"I suppose . . . these other scars on you, they're bullet wounds too, aren't they?"

"I'm afraid so."

"I suppose in your line of work it's bound to happen," Jean said. She was threading a needle that looked big enough to stitch up a Thanksgiving turkey.

"In my . . . yes, in my line it happens." He had forgotten briefly that he was Marshal J.T. Forsberg. That musn't be allowed to happen again. "If you're lucky, it happens more than once."

"I don't understand that. Oh—" enlightenment came. "Oh, yes. It couldn't happen more than once if . . . I see." She came to Shell with the thread and needle and he looked into the fire and far away, not caring to think about this too much. He had been sewn up before and hadn't yet learned to like it.

"Would you like a glass of whisky first? My brother keeps a jug somewhere."

"No," Morgan said. "No, thanks."

That explained the man. There was a brother, and somehow that made Shelter feel better about things, helped him to ignore the painful workings of the needle as it was pushed through nerve-filled flesh.

It also helped to think about Marshal Forsberg. He had taken a hell of a lot more than a needle and thread. Someone had tied him up and then deliberately cut him to pieces with a knife. Someone quite sadistic, quite savage. For what reason? Just for the fun of it, perhaps, and that was frightening, truly frightening.

Shell watched Jean work, her eyes were intent, her lips pursed. She breathed in and out with that special cadence of concentration, her fingers moving deftly.

"I should have taken the whisky," Shell complained.

"That one went too deep."

"That one went too deep," he agreed.

"I'm almost done."

"Good. I think I am too." Shell wiped the perspiration from his forehead. It had suddenly gotten awfully hot in the small room. His head was beginning to be a little light too. His whole body throbbed with a steady pulse.

"This makes me feel awful," Jean said. "It really does, marshal, I swear it to you."

"It doesn't make me feel too good."

"I might have killed you."

"That's right. Any time you pick up a gun there's a chance of that. Respect those things, woman."

"To think I wrote to Denver for you," she said, shaking her head. She was through with the stitching now and after swabbing the wound off with carbolic, she began winding a bandage around the upper arm, around Shell's neck and back across his shoulder. The work was competent, the bandage tight but not unnecessarily so—she had done this work before, Morgan thought.

"I sent for you," she went on, "and then after waiting, hoping all this time that someone would show up in response to my letter, I nearly kill you when you do arrive. What a fool I was."

"Just a little quick on the trigger."

She crossed the room with her bandages, her bowl, her needle and thread, scissors and carbolic. She spoke from the kitchen.

"It's no excuse, I don't suppose, but this last year everyone who has set foot on this ranch has been an enemy. It's been terrible, and Bill and I have gotten more than a little edgy. Speaking for myself it's gotten near to panic," she laughed nervously.

"Bill's your brother."

"That's right." Jean emerged from the kitchen, wiping her hands on a red and white towel. "He came up last year from Arkansas to help me out after things got . . . just got too tough for me to handle. He didn't want to come, I know that. Bill was a merchant, a successful merchant down home, but he came anyway to do what he could. After my father died there wasn't a lot of heart left in me, I have to admit that."

"This was your father's ranch."

"That's right. He and I came out together during the war. Joshua Waltham was his name."

"What happened to him?" Shell asked. He was putting his shirt back on, watching the fire, the slender back of the woman across the room as he did so.

"The night riders," she said with a shrug. "At least I think it was them. Who else could have done it? I found the door open in the middle of the night. Pa's boots were under the chair, his hat on the wall peg. But he was outside!

"I went out, and, marshal, I had a gun in my hands that night too. They had been taking our cattle, taking them, butchering them before anyone could see a brand, selling them to the mine owners. Pa was raising hell—he had an idea or two who it was behind this, where their hideout was."

She was silent for a second. She shrugged and smiled weakly. "Well, I found Pa. Shot up. Out along the trail. The night riders did it and I was alone, all alone. I guess they figured I'd pull off then, but I'm not cut that way. I wrote for Bill and he showed up, bless him. Then I wrote to the marshal's office and they sent you. Well, now there's three of us. Maybe we can teach them a lesson."

"Sure," Shelter was thinking. "Now there's three of us against a band of cutthroat killers." What the hell kind of lesson were they going to teach anyone? It hurt to look into the eyes of that blue-eyed woman-child and see the trust and faith there. She had gone and gotten herself a marshal. To her mind that had accomplished something. The marshal, he supposed, was supposed to be able to ride into the hills, take on a band of armed killers and mete out punishment. Well, the marshal was dead, and there was only Shelter Morgan. And what the hell was he doing involved in all of this? He had come for one man and now he was wrapped up in a territory-wide war against a gang of brigands. A wise man would have upped and ridden then and there.

But there was the girl and she turned those trusting eyes on Morgan—blue eyes, wide eyes, trusting eyes, eyes that waited for hope, and Morgan, shrugging heavily, said:

"Get me some dinner, Jean. We've got a lot of talking to do."

6.

The lady was a fair cook. As the thunder rumbled outside and the darkness of evening settled in Jean Waltham served up a helping of beef and pinto beans, cornbread and mustard greens to Shelter Morgan who sat facing the girl across the table, listening to her story of what had been going on, and continued to go on around Hogan, Colorado.

"They do what they want," she said with an exasperated sigh. "If they want beef they take it. If they can get their hands on your gold, they put it in their pockets. The people around here are plain buffaloed. Half of them think the night riders are heroic; the other half are plain scared."

"They spread a little of that money around, do they?" Morgan asked.

"Sure! If they've got a hundred head of cattle and they leave one at some shanty farm, why those people will swear forever that the night riders are the greatest men that ever rode down the pike. Hell—of course they never bother the poor folks! What the hell have the poor folks got that they want!"

"And you . . ."

"And me, I'm working on becoming poor," Jean said. "I'm working on it real fast, Marshal Forsberg. If I lose many more steers I just won't have anything left after I sell this year's herd. Not enough to pay off the bank, to pay the drovers I'll need to move my cattle. It's gotten down to this: either the night riders leave or my brother and I will have to."

The voice came from the doorway behind Shell: "And we're not leaving."

Morgan turned his head a quarter to look toward the door. A man of medium height stood there. He wore a yellow rain slicker and carried a rifle. Behind him the rain fell through the murky darkness. The man came in and kicked the door shut behind him.

"Who the hell's this?" he demanded.

"Bill, this is the marshal. Marshal J.T. Forsberg from Denver."

"It is, is it? You mean they actually sent someone?" Bill Waltham crossed the room, trailing water. He propped his rifle up in the corner and Shelter relaxed.

"I told you they'd send someone, they had to, didn't they?" Jean was a little flustered. This had been a hard day for her. She apparently didn't want her brother to give her a hard time as well. Shelter felt a little sorry for her. A frightened woman spending much time alone in these hills, she had fired too quickly and he had made it rough on her.

She had made coffee to go with supper and Bill Waltham, squatting down near the hearth, poured himself a cup. He had dark green eyes which now measured up Shelter Morgan. There was mistrust or doubt or uneasiness in those eyes—Shell couldn't decide which, but he didn't blame the man for any of it. He too had been hoeing a tough row, apparently.

"You've got some identification, I suppose."

"That's right," Morgan answered.

"Oh, Bill," Jean said peevishly, "can't you see the badge he's wearing?"

"Badge don't mean a thing," Bill Waltham said accurately "Anyone can pin one one."

"There's papers in my coat," Shell said. "And the letter from your sister."

"Let's see them," Bill Waltham said. He was standing now, coffee cup in one hand—his left hand—and he was eyeing Shelter narrowly. Morgan stood and walked to the other chair, not taking his eyes from Bill Waltham who watched with intensity. Waltham still held that coffee cup in his left hand, and his right rested near the butt of his holstered pistol. Merchant or not, Bill Waltham knew a trick or two.

Shelter walked to where the man stood and held out the letter, the identification he had taken from J.T. Forsberg's pockets. The warrant he held on to.

Waltham scanned the letter and other papers quickly, his eyes flickering to Shelter Morgan. "They let you men wear a beard, do they?"

"They let me. I've worn this one for years."

"You wouldn't think they would."

"Then you'd be wrong," Morgan said patiently. He stuck out his hand for the papers. "You through with those?"

"I reckon," Waltham said in a tone which was neither pleased nor certain. "What's my sister been telling you?" he asked, giving Jean a hard glance.

"Just a little about the night riders, something about your troubles, your father's death."

"Yes, and Jean talks too much," Bill said.

62

"Why, what would you have me do?" the girl said, firing up. "Clam up after calling the marshal all the way up here from Denver? Keep things a secret from him? Besides, everyone knows what I've told him, Bill. He probably had heard most of it before." She looked at Shell for assistance.

"That's right. I've heard most of it before. All except what happened to your father."

"Told you that too, did she!" For a moment there Bill Waltham was truly angry. Why, Morgan couldn't have guessed, but he looked ready to blow a fuse. The look he gave his sister could have withered her.

"It don't mean anything, Bill," Jean said quietly.

"Why you darned fool, it means . . ."

"It don't mean a thing," she said again and slowly Bill Waltham calmed himself.

"No. It's all right, It's just that things are so damned stirred up all the time around here. It's like walking barefoot over broken bottles. A man gets sly and close-mouthed. Sorry," he said with an apologetic shrug.

"All right," Shell said. "Don't think anything of it. The question here's not what happened, after all, but what we're going to do to fix it, and that's going to require the three of us to work together. I suggest we start to do just that."

First things being first, Bill and Shelter sat down at the table and Waltham sketched a map of the country for "the marshal", using an old piece of brown wrapping paper from the general store.

"The Big Dome is above the town itself and the low valleys. That's where all of the gold strikes have been. If you've been to Hogan, you've seen the dome. A big barren mountain criss-crossed by mine roads now."

"I've seen it."

"Good. You've got the dome and the town at its foot. On the other side of the Big Dome is Calamity

Valley. Named so for a party of westward rolling folks who wintered up there and starved to death. That is where the Double O and the Cinch Ring are—two of the biggest ranches, two that have been hit the hardest by the night riders."

Shelter nodded. He was watching the map and Bill Waltham with one eye, the woman with the other. She was cleaning up in the kitchen, her movements quick, practised.

"Stretching south from the Big Dome are the Little Utes. They run to about six thousand feet at the highest. You can just see the shoulders of them beyond the timber. This side of the watershed is us, the JW, and the half dozen little ranches, the Kiowa, the Square Knot, the D slant K, ZZ, Rafter T, Circle L. All in here, in these lower valleys." Bill Waltham circled the lower areas on the eastern slopes of the Little Ute Range.

"That's about it," he said, settling back in his chair. "The trails, the ins and outs, the canyons, a man can't learn overnight, but that's the way she sets up in general."

"Uh-huh." Morgan was sitting there looking at the map still, trying to fix it in his mind. "One thing troubles me, Walthan. There's what, eight ranches here and about? They must each hire three to five men, maybe a dozen. Why isn't that enough to keep these night riders at bay?"

"You answer that for me, will you, marshal. I'm damned if I know. Working wages aren't good enough, I suppose. Maybe these cowboys can't make up their minds that a dollar a day is worth dying for. What do you make, marshal?"

"Not a great deal more."

"No. Maybe you understand it then. I don't. All I know is that most places you go the good folks outnumber the bad, but the bad get their way. Why is that?''

Shell said he guessed he didn't know.

"Oh for God's sake, Bill," Jean said peevishly. "Why don't you make up your mind to tell the marshal?"

"Hush, Jean." His dark green eyes flashed a warning at the woman.

Undaunted Jean Waltham walked toward her brother. The fire snapped and popped behind her as the flames found a knot. Outside the rain continued. Shell could hear the whistling wind in the eaves of the cabin, but he paid little attention to it. His eyes, his hearing were fixed on Bill Waltham. The man had his secrets, it appeared. He did have his secrets. He wasn't thrilled to have the law in his house—or what he took to be the law.

"What's she want to tell me, Bill?" Shell asked mildly.

"It's nothing."

Shell nodded and walked to the fire himself. Turning his back to the fire, warming his hands, he asked, "Does this have anything to do with the men who were here this afternoon?"

It was a shot in the dark, but it touched home. Bill Waltham looked briefly like he would catapult out of that chair, but he regained control.

"What men?" he asked in a low voice.

"Come on, Bill, it was a simple question."

"You were spying on us."

"Spying, hell. I saw the tracks of their horses. I thought it might be something I needed to know about so I asked."

Waltham was sprawled comfortably in his wooden chair, his legs stretched out before him, his spine supporting him. He was slouched down so low that his handgun was in easy reach, his draw unhampered.

Shelter noticed that as he had noticed Bill Waltham drinking coffee with his left hand. Waltham was no fool. He might be playing the rancher, the city man come West, the ex-merchant, but Bill Waltham had been down the trail before. He had seen some fighting somewhere, Shell was willing to bet.

"Tell him, Bill." Jean said it softly. Her eyes implored her brother. "The marshal's going to get the wrong idea, Bill." Jean glanced once at Shell, a fleeting smile tilting her lips. "After all, I've already shot him."

"I can't, damnit! Decatur'll have my hide."

"No. He'll understand."

"He will, will he! You don't know Lewis Decatur like I do, Jean. His word is meant to be taken as law."

"But Mister Forsberg is the law—the real law," Jean insisted.

"Yes," Bill sighed. "I know that." The kid folded his fingers together and sat peering over them at Shelter Morgan, trying to read something in those cold blue eyes.

"Let's have it, Bill. Save yourself a lot of trouble."

"That's what I'm trying to do," he replied sharply, "I just ain't sure how to go about it."

"Let's work it out together," Shell said.

"All right." Bill Waltham stood and sighed deeply, shrugging "Get my whisky jug, will you, Jean? Thanks."

Waltham stood looking past Shell at the fire, not saying anything for a long minute. Jean returned with a jug of liquor, pulled the cork and gave each man a short slug of it in a tin coffee cup. Her breasts brushed Shelters's shoulder as she placed the whiskey in his hands. Their eyes met for an instant, then Shelter turned his attention back to Bill.

Shelter waited patiently. The man was worried. He

downed his whisky in a gulp.

"Decatur'll kill me."

"You already said that," Jean commented peevishly. She had settled down in the corner to do some mending, her sewing basket on her lap.

"All right," Waltham said taking a slow breath, "this is it—you've asked about the people around here, why they didn't band together and stand up to the night riders. Well, what if they did decide to do that?"

"It would be illegal," Shell said. "Strictly speaking, it's illegal to form a vigilante group."

"You're a lawman, aren't you?" Waltham asked belligerently. He took a step nearer Shell, his jaw clenched.

"Easy. Look, Bill, I'm wearing a badge but I don't have a legal or moral mandate to report or arrest, to interfere with people who are trying to defend themselves."

"I told you," Jean said triumphantly.

"It's easy to say that," Bill shot back. "How do we know what you'll do?"

"You don't."

"We have to work in secrecy, marshal. If one of us is identified, why his life isn't worth living. The night riders have no conscience whatever. They'll burn a man's home, cut his throat and take his wife in the bargain. People know that. It's been hell just getting men to stand up with us. They won't take lightly to being exposed."

"No." They wouldn't. As Bill Waltham had pointed out, they had the night riders on the one side against them, the law on the other. The vigilance group would ride wary. Shelter thought he had a solution. "I can give you folks a kind of protection, Bill," he suggested.

"What are you talking about! What could you do for us?"

"Listen, you darn fool," Jean said, looking up from her mending. Her voice was sharp, but there was a softness in her eyes as she looked at Shelter, looked deeply.

"It's this way, Bill. I'm carrying the law's authority. You men can be carrying it too. I'll deputize you one and all if I can meet with your people and I like what I see."

"No!" Bill's voice was a shout.

"Why not?"

"Decatur'll have my hide, I swear he will. Look, Marshal Forsberg, I've already admitted everything. I've broken the code, you see."

"I see, and if this thing gets out of hand and you men start riding over this territory lynching everyone you suspect, everyone with a Southern accent, every stranger you meet, what have you got then? A damned war is what it is. All of you on both sides riding masked, afraid to be recognized, all of you shooting first, out to kill. I don't know how you're going to be able to tell the good from the bad in the end, Bill. You people have the right idea, but you need some control."

"And you're it?"

"I'm it," Shell answered, his eyes cool and hard, his teeth clenched.

Bill tossed his hands into the air and turned away. "And if I take you down there, they'll know my word's no good."

"When's the meeting, Bill? Tonight?"

"How did you . . . ?" Waltham was amazed, but it hadn't taken a lot of guesswork. Those riders had come by the isolated JW Ranch for some purpose. Why else than to inform Bill of a meeting?

"Maybe I could just show up," Morgan said.

"No." Bill wagged his head heavily. "I'll take you with me. Everything you've said is true. Some of the boys are getting a little wild already. They're nervous and angry all at once. They're liable to hurt someone that they don't mean to hurt. They need control."

"What about this Decatur? I thought he was in charge. Can't he control them, Bill?"

"If he wanted to, I guess—well, wait until you meet Lewis Decatur, you'll see what I mean. He's one of the big mine owners up on the Dome, one of the hardest hit. He don't care so much about controlling his people as getting his revenge." Bill was still worried. Thoughtfully he said, "This had better work out, marshal. Things had better be as you say they are. If they aren't, well—I wouldn't want to be in your shoes."

"But you are, Bill," Shelter said with a nasty little smile. "We're in this together now, old friend. Where I go, you go. You're bringing me into the vigilantes and if Decatur doesn't like us, why I guess he'll do what he can to take care that neither of us ever carries word of this out of the mountains."

Bill didn't like that, he didn't like it a bit, but he swallowed it. He had to.

"You can't blame him for being worried," Jean Waltham said. They stood together under the eaves of the cabin, watching the rain slant down. Shelter wore a rain slicker. He held the reins to the big roan in one hand, his rifle in the other.

"No, I don't blame him," Shelter said. "But he's got to do this my way. And the same goes for Decatur."

"Don't push on Lewis Decatur, marshal."

"No? I push where I need to, Jean. Generally something gives."

"He's a big man, a powerful man, used to having his own way, marshal."

"We all have to be disappointed sometime," was Morgan's comment.

He was thinking the situation through, trying to measure it. It didn't have a good feel. If everything went right he could find himself leading an army, an army capable of riding down the outlaws and stopping them cold. And with that army was Kyle Cornelius, the man who was waiting for the retribution Shelter carried with him.

If things went wrong, they could go very wrong. Morgan wasn't a lawman and someone around here knew it. Knew it because they had already killed Marshal J.T. Forsberg once. If this thing blew up in Shell's face he would find himself between two armies, the vigilantes of Lewis Decatur and Cornelius's night riders. And he hadn't an ally in all of the mountains.

Well, maybe one.

"You come back," Jean whispered into his ear as they stood together watching the darkness and the rain. She leaned near to him and her hand darted inside of his slicker to drop to his crotch. Cupping his groin in her hand she pressed herself against him, tasting his lips. "You be sure you come back to see me, marshal —no matter what."

7.

It had stopped raining half an hour later. A silver dollar moon floated through the high broken clouds, edging them with mercury. It was suddenly very cold. The grass was frozen beneath the horses' hoofs, and it crackled as they trod it down. The hills were dark and endless. There wasn't a sound but the creaking of saddle leather, the clink of bridle chains, the blowing of the horses as they moved down the trail tossing their heads, breathing out great steamy clouds.

Bill Waltham was in no mood for talking and Shelter didn't push it. There was plenty of time later for that. The lights of Hogan came into view. Tiny winking fireflies against the prevailing blackness. Two dozen lanterns at most. Only the saloons were open. The rest of the town slept on, dreaming of the next big gold strike.

Waltham walked his horse up and out of the gulley and onto the main road. He glanced once at Shelter as if he would say something, but he clamped his jaw shut again and rode on.

They approached the brick house from behind, walking their horses through the trees. A light burned in one window upstairs, in three or four down. The trees cast dark moving shadows against the house.

There were easily a dozen horses standing around hitched among the trees. To Shell's right was a brick barn and he would have bet there were many more horses waiting there.

"Quite a gathering," Shelter said.

"Shh!" Bill turned sharply in the saddle, his eyes too-bright, frightened. "We'll leave our mounts here," he whispered, swinging down.

Shell hitched his roan to the low limb of a cottonwood and followed Bill through the trees toward the massive two-story house ahead of them. Apparently owning a mine was a paying proposition, Morgan thought, eyeing the house.

"Halt!" the hoarse whisper from Shell's left said, and his hand automatically dropped toward his holstered Colt before he could stop himself. "That's it," the whisper said again. "You almost made a serious mistake there, mister. Who are you?"

"It's Bill Waltham. That you, Jed?"

"It's me. Who's with you?"

"New hand." Bill was nervous. His voice jumped, the guard didn't notice it. He was probably more concerned about keeping warm on what had become a bitterly cold night suddenly. "He's all right."

"Go ahead then. Most everyone's already inside."

Bill led off, his back stiff. His muscles were rigid with apprehension. Bill Waltham wasn't liking this a good deal.

They approached the back door of the house. A solid, white-painted wooden door with nice brass fittings. In the window above them another guard sat with a rifle on his lap looking out at the dark yard.

Bill knocked three times then once more and the door swung open. Shelter followed him in past a frowning man in a town suit, a one-eyed man with a thatch of red hair which sprouted up wildly in all directions.

It was warmer now. Voices sounded in murmuring unison behind a set of white double doors across the room. Men stood up and down the corridor, against the walls, looking grim and determined.

Many of them seemed to be miners, which figured. The boss would have ordered them onto this job. There were others who were just as obviously cowhands or storekeepers. One frail, chalky man could have been a preacher but for the big Colt riding on his hip. He was as pale as an albino this one, but his eyes were dark, very dark in contrast to his pale, fine hair. He eyed Shelter Morgan with considerable interest.

"All right, gentlemen," someone said. "Let's go in. Mister Decatur is ready for us."

The double doors were opened and men started pressing that way. Shell walked through, finding himself in a huge, red-carpeted room where chairs had been set up. Standing in the front of the room was a silver-haired man with a flowing mustache, a broad bay window, the ruddy cheeks of a drinking man, the heavy fists of a fighter. He was Shell's height and much heavier though older by quite a few years.

Shell was looking at the kingpin and he knew it. Lewis Decatur stood near his mahogany desk looking out at the lesser men. Men he could buy and sell or whip barehanded.

On Decatur's right hand was a tall, narrow, smirking kid of twenty or twenty-one.

"Who's that?" Shell asked Bill Waltham.

"Decatur's son. Regis Decatur." Bill's voice was

tight. There were beads of perspiration along his eyebrows.

"And that?" Shell asked, for someone infinitely more interesting had appeared on Decatur's left. She was tall, poised, her auburn hair done up in coils and ringlets, her eyes haughty and cool, her figure remarkable, her breasts milky and smooth where they showed above the white gown she wore. A diamond necklace encircled her delicate throat. Her eyes shuttled across the room, passed by Shelter Morgan and seemed to return of their own volition.

"That," Bill Waltham managed to say, "is Gloria Decatur—an invitation to a lynch rope of your own, if you get me. Decatur won't stand for it, so don't get any ideas, marshal."

"I wouldn't," Morgan said with a straight face, "entertain such low thoughts."

The girl whispered something into her father's ear, got a stern look of disapproval in return and then was pointed out of the room. The old man watched her go, watched the door close behind her and then held up his hand for silence. His eyes now were on Morgan as well. A stranger at a party like this was bound to be noticed. Shell had been tagged.

"If we're going to get up to the Ute Trail," someone nearer the front said, "we'd better get this done with and get going. We all know our positions."

"One minute," Decatur said. His eyes were definitely on Shelter now. Damnit, the girl had nailed him down and tipped off the old man. The kid at his side looked positively anxious to use that Colt he had strapped to his thigh. Morgan watched the kid with some interest, but not much. This was no place for gunplay no matter how anxious a man was. The only interest Morgan had in guns on this night was the possibility of finding one with silver inlay, and that was a very remote chance at this gathering.

"I don't want to push, Mr. Decatur . . ." the man in front began again.

"Then don't, Logan! We've business to take care of here first. That gold shipment doesn't even leave until midnight."

Logan, was it? That was Sailor Logan in front then, and Morgan lifted up on his toes to get a better look at the man—lean, bristly chin chiskers, torn flop hat, leather coat over a quilted vest. The resemblance to Daltry Logan was there, but you had to look for it. Daltry was soft, his features blurred, Sailor looked to be all barrel staves and leather.

Bill Waltham's elbow touched Shelter in the ribs. Morgan looked back to the big man, to Lewis Decatur whose eyes were still on Shell.

"Boys, we've had some word of what we've planned leak out. It was so bad that we missed the night riders completely at the ZZ Ranch. If we hadn't gone half an hour earlier to Joe Pearl's place they would have burned him out last week. There's someone among us talking, men. That's all there is to it, and it pains me to think or say it—but we've got a traitor among us."

"'Look to the Rebs," someone said. "You know damn well it's a Reb if we got a traitor. There's not more'n a handful of 'em with us."

"Look here, John Cody . . ." Sailor Logan began fiercely. Decatur cut him off.

"It doesn't follow that it's a Reb, John. Look at Sailor here, we all know he stood up to the night riders. We all know another thing or two he did which shows where he stands." Which meant, Morgan figured, that there was a night rider buried somewhere. Credit to Sailor Logan.

"Yeah, well, you know no one from the Dome is standing with them night riders," the big man, Cody, growled.

Morgan listened to this with a part of his attention while the other followed the course of the narrow, flaxen-haired man across the room. He had seen the man outside, the one who resembled a preacher more than a badman, but had the feel about him of a very, very dangerous hombre. The pistol he wore was at fingertip length, tied down. He wore black, again emphasizing the resemblance to a preacher man—or to an undertaker.

He was slowly working his way across the room. When Shell had first seen him he had been leaning against the wall near the doorway. Now he was halfway toward the front, standing looking at the floor, his hands clasped together. He was getting himself into position. Shell opened his rain slicker but did nothing else. Bill Waltham shot him an uneasy glance. The kid was pale, very pale.

"The fact remains that we have a security problem," Lewis Decatur continued. "And we just can't afford that, gentlemen. We just can't. This is a war for survival. The survival of our businesses, of our woman and children, our ranches, and we cannot risk losing this war."

He did it so suddenly that poor Bill Waltham nearly toppled over in his anxiety. Decatur was looking at the men in the front row, smiling that reassuring politician's smile of his. Then suddenly his eyes went to Bill Waltham, to Morgan standing beside him, and Shelter noticed that the Preacher was much nearer now, three men away, behind them, his hand resting carelessly near his gun.

"Who is this you've brought to us, Bill Waltham!" Decatur's voice boomed out and the kid's mouth twisted in a slow, silent curse.

"If we could speak to you, sir."

"Of course, Bill," Decatur answered easily. "First I want to know just who in hell I am talking to, however; who the hell have you brought to see us, Bill?"

The kid, Regis Decatur, was slavering as if the old man had brought him something good to eat. The Preacher was practically at Shell's shoulder, and Morgan had decided that he would allow the man no nearer. Lewis Decatur was leaning forward from the waist, his eyes fixed on Bill Waltham who seemed incapable of speech.

"I'm a United States Marshal," Shelter said, striding toward the front of the room. A murmur rose around him. Someone grabbed at his coat sleeve, but Shell knocked the hand away. "My name is J.T. Forsberg," he announced, flashing the badge he had pinned to his shirt, "and I'm here to save you all from making a lot of trouble for yourselves."

"A marshal," Decatur said with a loud sniff. His son, at his shoulder, laughed out loud, a hollow, stupid laugh.

"That's what I said, Decatur. And you men are gathered here illegally right now, and you know it."

"Conspiracy to riot? To commit murder?"

"We don't have to start defining it. You know what you're up to. You know it's outside the law to proceed in this manner."

"Tell it to my wife," someone up front bellowed. "You just go up to her grave and tell her that we're proceeding against the law. You let the night riders kill her and yet you want to stop us from doing justice. And damn you, Bill Waltham for bringing this badge-toting bastard with you!"

"Easy," Morgan said. They had begun to surge forward toward the desk where Shelter stood beside Decatur and his huge dumb puppy of a son.

"Easy, hell. Badge or none, you've got a problem,

mister!"

"So have you, my friend, if you hinder a US marshal in the performance of his duty."

"What about our duty? What about hindering us as we try to protect ourselves from these night riders?"

There was a moment's general tumult and Morgan waited for it to subside before he said quietly, firmly. "Men, I'm not here to stop you. And you can quit blaming Bill Waltham for bringing me here. He's shown a bit of common sense, that's all."

"What are you talking about?"

"You'd better explain yourself, marshal," Lew Decatur said in a tone of voice which indicated he had plenty of cards left to play.

"I'd be happy to explain myself if you boys would settle down and let me," Morgan said. "You've got a problem here and no one has done much to help you. All right—I'm here to help you. One little woman with gumption and brains wrote to the marshal's office in Denver. I mean Jean Waltham. She's the only one in this whole damned territory, as near as I can tell, who had the sense to go about things the right way."

"What's that—your way?"

"Yes, it is. That's right. The law's way."

"I seen this man around town a few days ago," someone said. "He didn't say a thing about bein' a marshal. How the hell do we know who he is?"

Without switching his eyes, Morgan handed the papers J.T. Forsberg had carried to Lewis Decatur who scanned them making small noises in his throat.

"It looks good to me," Decatur had to say after a minute, handing the papers back to Shell. "That doesn't mean you're wanted here, mister."

"It means I'm needed here, damn you," Morgan went on, pushing it hard. Is that the way J.T. Forsberg would have told it? Maybe. Shell knew that he would have if he were a Marshal. But was there someone out there who *knew* he wasn't Forsberg? "I'm here to bail you out, Decatur, to take this slippery little idea of yours and make it into something noble and very legal, to take this dark thing and turn the light on it, to keep the whole lot of you on the legal side of a hanging rope."

"What are you talking about!" It was the kid, Regis Decatur who started screaming. "We don't need you for nothing! This is my Pa's town, my Pa's posse! We don't need a two-bit federal marshal horning in here and telling us how to do our job!" The kid had a mouth on him; he also didn't have a lick of sense. He went for his holstered pistol and Shelter Morgan was all over him like a big cat, taking the barrel of the pistol, the kid's wrist and making the angle between them an inch or two the other side of comfort. The kid screamed out as bone grated against nerve and the iron clattered to the floor.

"Let go of him, damn you!" Lewis Decatur said, and his voice had more menace in it than the kid could raise in a lifetime. He was the bull of the woods and he would kill if he got started. Kill efficiently, quickly, without qualms, and Shelter Morgan knew it. He knew it, but he wasn't buffaloed by it. He had spent most of his lifetime among people who were equipped for killing in one way or another.

Shelter kicked the pistol away. It skidded across the floor and thunked against the baseboard of the opposite wall. "The kid's not old enough for such toys," Morgan said. "I'd keep them out of his hand."

"You touch my boy again . . . damn you, I'll have you, Forsberg."

"Train your boy. It beats hell out of trying to structure the rest of the world so that it'll accept a thing like he is."

Lewis Decatur turned red and then crimson. Then he took a series of deep, slow breaths and his color returned to normal. His voice was soft when he spoke again, and then, Morgan knew, the man was truly dangerous. He had never feared the wild ones, the savage ones, but those who could coldly take hate into their nests and nurture it—they were the frightening ones.

"What is it you're proposin'?" Sailor Logan asked, breaking the deadly mood. He was a shrewd looking narrow man past his middle years. He wore scraggly chin whiskers and carried a long rifle. There was the mark of the mountains on him.

"I want to join you," Shelter said. "I want you men to take me in. I want this gang broken up as much as you do, more perhaps."

"Let you in. Then you've got the evidence against us," a big red-bearded man said.

"Let me in and there's no evidence to be had. I mean to deputize all of you." A murmur ran around the room again. "That's right. Every last one of you. When you go hunting you'll be going legal."

"That means we'll have to let them off light," a man to Shell's right put in.

"It means they'll not be lynched, yes. They can be brought to town and held, tried legally and then justice can be meted out." There was a deal of subdued conversation. Decatur pointed out the obvious to his people.

"Men, we start bringing the night riders into town for trial, we've got a problem. They'll come in looking for their own, and half the country's on their side, damnit. The half that has the idea these boys are fighting for the glory of the South or some such. We're liable to have our town burned down around our ears.

"On the other hand," he admitted with a sigh, "I don't know what we can do in the face of a United

States Marshal's presence but follow his lead. I don't like it, but I suppose that'll have to be it.

"As far as the night riders finding out who we are individually, well, it already seems pretty clear to me that we've got a traitor among us. I don't think we're risking much there . . . but I'll warn that traitor, whoever he is," Decatur's eyes raked the gathered men, "when I find you the marshal won't be around to see what happens, and what happens will be plain nasty. I guess that's clear to everyone. Let's get to the plan—" he paused and then said as if it had suddenly occurred to him, "where did you say you were from, Marshal Forsberg? Isn't there a touch of old Dixie in that accent of yours?"

"Maybe a trace," Shelter shrugged. "I'm from Kentucky. I fought with the 16th Ohio, though. Sorry—I've always been a Union man and I still am. You ought to know a rebel couldn't carry a federal badge."

"Sorry—just curiosity," Decatur said. "My brother was 16th Ohio, as a matter of fact. Colonel Trask's second in command."

"Was he," Shelter said just as casually. "Funny, the four years I was there Colonel DeCourcey was commanding the 16th. Wonder what outfit your brother had gotten himself attached to. Could be he was fighting on the wrong side and never realized it."

A rumble of laughter followed that remark and Decatur even allowed himself a smile, though Junior, standing to one side, still rubbing his wrist didn't even come near it.

"We're decided then," Decatur said. "Let's get on with this business, men. We're wasting time."

Shell resumed his original position next to Bill Waltham. The Preacher, he noticed, had drifted casually away to lean against the wall, but there was a look in the pale man's eyes, an almost merry look, if twin stones like the Preacher had for eyes can show happiness. He knew, oh yes, he knew.

Shell had gotten his foot in the door. The vigilantes had accepted him, for the time being.

For the time being he was one of them, and they were going to ride together to stop the night riders because it was convenient. There would come a time when it was not so convenient to have Shelter Morgan around. Then they would kill him. He knew that.

The Preacher continued to smile.

8.

"The gold shipment's a dud, but no one outside of this room knows that. No one's been told until right now." Lewis Decatur was pulling on a dark rain slicker as he addressed the vigilantes. "When that wagon rolls out at midnight from my mine office it'll look like the real thing. More, since there will be an additional three guards with it. Travelling at midnight will make it look all the more authentic."

Decatur finished buttoning his slicker. He put on a dark hat and took a Winchester from his son's hand, levering a round into the chamber, lowering the hammer.

"We'll be on the old Ute trail, men. That's the way I'm sending the wagon. Not much of a road, barely passable for a wagon. Those boys riding with it are going to have a hell of a time tonight.

"By now, knowing we've got a traitor among us, I

expect the night riders are ready to hit that gold shipment. But we're going to be there first. When that wagon comes rolling up the Ute trail, we're going to be in the hills with guns in our hands. And when those night riders make their try, boys, we're going to cut them to ribbons . . . if the marshal,'' he said with a slight bow, ''doesn't disapprove.''

"We'll do what has to be done to protect your property. That wagon is yours and you've got the right to keep it out of outlaw hands whether it's carrying gold or pig iron. All of you better poke your hands in the air now," Shelter told them. "It's a short oath, but it'll go a long way toward keeping you out of law trouble."

Or it would have if Morgan was J.T. Forsberg. He had to play it exactly as if he was Forsberg. The slightest slip and he was a goner. Decatur had no use for him whatsoever.

". . . uphold the laws of the United States of America," the rumbling chorus of male voices finished and Shelter nodded to Lewis Decatur.

"All right, Decatur, let's get us some night riders."

That brought a spontaneous cheer. They turned in unison and started toward their horses, tramping through the the house, Shelter in their midst. He didn't miss anything as he headed out. He wanted to know where the windows were, the hallways, the doors, and staircases. It was possible he would be coming back here one dark night.

He took it all in, noticing the small things, the grandfather clock in the parlor, the sideboard where the whisky stood in decanters. And passing the staircase—the auburn haired, haughty woman standing looking down at them, her arms folded, her chin tilted up, her expression unreadable. Gloria Decatur—maybe she was disappointed that they hadn't killed Morgan after she had pointed him out to her father. Why had she done it? Did she have a grudge against the law, the night riders, traitors or men with beards? Morgan made himself a promise to find out.

Outside it was freezing, the stars crisp and bright in an inky sky. The trees stood together, frozen and unmoving. Starlight glossed the frozen dew on the grass.

"You'd better just ride alone," Bill Waltham said.

"Got no heart for it, Bill?"

"There's going to be some shooting tonight, Forsberg. Some people are more likely to be hit than others."

Shell swung up onto his roan's back, "Have you heard something, Bill, are are you just walking light?"

"Figure it out yourself, *marshal*," Bill said, and Morgan didn't like the emphasis. Waltham yanked his horse's head around and walked it off through the trees to join the main party.

"Make friends easy, don't you?" a scratchy voice said. A dry chuckle followed.

"Is that you, Sailor?"

"Yes," the man drawled. "How'd you come to know my name?"

"I keep my ears open."

"Do you? Was I you I'd keep my eyes open tonight too."

"Are they after me, Sailor?"

"Who?" the old man asked blankly.

"I guess you wouldn't be knowing."

"No, I wouldn't. I know two things tonight. I'm gettin' a chance to get some of my own back at these night riders and I'm your deputy."

"That's right. Why don't you stick close to me, Daltry, I don't want to get lost tonight."

"*Daltry?*" Sailor Logan's voice went tight and distant. "What's that you called me, Marshal Forsberg?"

"Why, I called you 'deputy', Logan," Shell said, cursing the quirk of his mind that had caused him to call Sailor by his brother's name. A brother Marshal J.T. Forsberg could never have heard of.

"I'll stick close, marshal," Sailor said at length, and the old man walked his horse up beside Shell to sit there, his rifle resting casually across the saddlebows, the muzzle on Shelter Morgan.

"I'll stick real close," Logan said again. "You don't have to worry about that."

From somewhere in front the signal was given and the horsemen moved out, thirty strong, the horses walking like dark ghosts through the trees. The town of Hogan was asleep now, even the saloons locked and silent. There was a light on against the hill above town, up on the Big Dome where the mines were. The gold shipment was being readied for the long run out to Leadville. And somewhere farther up in the hills an outlaw gang was lazily dressing, checking and rechecking weapons, saddling sleek horses, preparing itself for war.

Morgan rode forward to be beside Lewis Decatur who glanced at him without speaking. On the other side of the old man was Regis Decatur, his face a mask of tension. Lewis's baby boy wanted to get out there and put some lead in other men's bodies. Behind Decatur and to his left rode the Preacher. Narrow, pale, deadly. Shell had finally figured out where he had seen the man before—peering out at him from a poster in Utah. The name Morgan didn't recall. It wouldn't have been his real name anyway. But he was a bad one, a gun for hire. When you sell your gun you have to be very good with it and very willing to use it. The Preacher would be both.

The higher they rode the cooler it got. By the time they reached the old Ute trail Shell's bones felt brittle, frozen to the marrow, the flow of blood to ears, nose and extremities had long ago ceased.

Breath steamed from the nostrils of men and horses as they sat together on the narrow dark trail, catching a rest.

"Time?" Decatur whispered.

Someone struck a match and peered at a watch. "Eleven o'clock," a raspy voice answered.

"We're in good shape then. When you move off the road, move up, not down. If they want to run that way, let them. We'll keep the elevation. And get far back, far upslope. At least a hundred yards, leave the night riders room to occupy. Keep the horses quiet, and above all don't get impatient and start shooting. I'll fire first, all right? Questions?"

"How do you know they'll hit the wagon here, Decatur?" Morgan asked.

"Look around, marshal. Where the hell else? Down below there are bluffs on one side, a precipice on the other. No room to get off the trail and hide. Once you get up over the crest it's a flat run down to the meadows—and that eight horse team can pull that wagon like a bat out of hell. No, it's got to be here. You men get up into the brush, spread out good and wide. It'll be a long cold wait, but that doesn't mean there can be any smoking or talk. Sound will carry a long way on a night like this, boys. Keep it quiet."

They moved off upslope, dispersing into the brush and pine trees, the horses' hoofs clicking on stone, leather creaking, twigs breaking underfoot until at last they were all settled in and the night closed in around Shelter Morgan, a night as silent and dark and cold as any he had ever lived through.

He sat and waited patiently, his rifle in his hands as he had waited for many other battles, many other places. You sat and you waited, breathing in and out slowly, knowing that death was coming on silent wings. Death for you, for the enemy, for both. Somehow the mind cleared at those times and death didn't seem so very menacing after all.

We are here only to pass on anyway. In a hundred years it wouldn't matter much. You'd be gone anyway. Dying is the fulfillment of life, after all. There were millions of better men in the ground, more millions to come—it was in *how* you lived, how you died that a man defined himself, not in the act of living, the act of dying.

So Shelter sat and waited and the night was a cold menace parading silver stars past his eyes.

"I'm telling you," Sailor Logan was saying, "he's not up from Denver, or if he is, he's not been there long. He knows my brother, Daltry. Knows his name."

"Keep your voice down, damnit," Decatur hissed. He wouldn't have allowed Sailor Logan to talk at all, but this was something that interested him profoundly. He didn't like the smell of Marshal Forsberg himself.

"What are you talking about?" Decatur asked.

"What did I say? He called me by my brother's name back there, I swear to you he did." Sailor stood in the dark shadows of the pines facing Lewis Decatur. He didn't like Decatur, never had, but the mine boss was a strong ally in this fight against the night riders—a fight Sailor Logan couldn't afford to lose. He would have allied himself with the devil to keep his land and protect his two kids.

"You're sure?"

"He tried to cover it up, tried to say he had called me 'deputy', but it was Daltry sure as hell," Sailor Logan insisted.

"And your brother's in California."

"He has been for five years, that's right. Unless this

man who claims to be a Denver marshal knew him down home in Alabama, he's met Daltry in California recent."

"And he couldn't have met Daltry during the war— not if J.T. Forsberg was with the l6th Ohio."

"That's the way I was figuring it, Mister Decatur."

"All right, Sailor," Decatur said, placing a hand on Logan's shoulder. It was a gesture Sailor Logan didn't care for at all but he kept his mouth shut. "I'll see to the marshal."

Sure he would—there would be plenty of opportunity when the battle started. It would be impossible to tell who had hit who.

Decatur stood in the darkness pondering things for a while. Forsberg hadn't smelled right from the start. It was a hell of a time for a US marshal to show up, but there was a lot that didn't ring true about him—little things. The southern accent. The beard. The fact that Forsberg knew Logan's brother from somewhere. Small things. Enough to add up to a large doubt about Marshal J.T. Forsberg. Maybe he was the authentic lawman he represented himself to be, Decatur thought. It didn't matter. Forsberg, real or bogus, was in the way, a threat to Decatur's own plans.

"Preacher?"

The narrow man detached himself from the shadows and sidled up to the mine boss.

"Yes, Mr. Decatur."

"I want you to stay close to the marshal."

"Yes, sir."

"Very close, you get me?"

"I get you," the Preacher said with some relish.

"And when the shooting starts, you watch out for him, won't you, Preacher?"

"Leave it to me."

The Preacher sifted off then through the shadows, his

dark figure being swallowed up by the night. Decatur settled in to wait again. *That* at least was taken care of. If anything ever came of this the blame could be placed on the night riders. Let the US marshal's office move in in force then and wipe the bastards out.

"Dad."

Lewis Decatur grimaced with distaste in the darkness. It wasn't something he intended, but it was difficult to help. The kid was kinked somewhere. Decatur had tried to protect him; if anyone crossed Regis Decatur he would have the old man to deal with. But he had never had any affection for the boy—not the kind a father was supposed to have for a son. There was something decayed and vicious, rotten in the boy's guts.

"What do you want? Didn't I tell everyone to be quiet?" Decatur growled.

"Where's the Preacher going?"

"To piss in the woods. How the hell would I know?"

"You sent him after the marshal."

"Did I?"

"I want him, Dad. I want the marshal bad. I can handle the job myself." There was something puppyish about Regis just then. Puppyish and dirty. He wanted to kill, Lewis Decatur knew. He had always wanted to kill. As a child he had taken his pets and squeezed the life out of them, broken their necks, stabbed them . . . Regis and his sister. They were two of a kind. Little Gloria might even have been worse.

"I don't know where the Preacher went. Take up your position, keep quiet and keep your head down."

"Dad . . ."

"Did you hear me!"

"I heard you . . ." Regis started to add something else. His voice was sulky and low now.

"Mr. Decatur." Someone breathless and hurried rushed to where the father and son stood talking.

"What is it, Earl?"

"Heard something from the ridge, Mr. Decatur. Sounded like horses moving up through the arroyo."

"Night riders?"

"You tell me who else."

"Get into position. Everyone into position! And not a whisper, not a sound. Regis!" Decatur shoved his son aside, "Get back where I stationed you. Earl, tell the men down the line to listen for my shot. Watch for the gold wagon and then listen for my signal. Regis, damn you, what are you doing standing here. Get back up in the rocks."

There was a momentary scuffle, men rushing into the brush, hurried instructions, whispered curses, and then the night was silent again. Silent and death laden.

Regis Decatur turned and slowly headed back upslope. He walked past his position and on into the trees. He didn't give one damn about the night riders, about the gold they had stolen or would steal, about the dead men they would trample over. He had been insulted in front of thirty men. That was all that mattered—to end that affair with death. The marshal was below him but Regis climbed still higher, climbed into the mossy, ice-glossed rocks. The man would never suspect anyone to come from that side. The kill would be an easy one and honor would be satisfied. He only wanted to beat the Preacher to it. Why should the Preacher get all the credit? Why should that little slime have the reputation he had? He wasn't any bigger or stronger or faster than Regis Decatur. On this night Regis meant to show his father that he was a man, to show the Preacher and that cold-eyed marshal, to show Gloria who had always laughed . . . Regis saw the movement below, saw the marshal waiting in ambush and he settled in to wait for his chance. When the guns began to speak it would be time. The shot was an easy one. Downslope two hundred feet, a few obstructing trees, but no problem there—he was a dead man, was Marshal J.T. Forsberg. Dead and finished.

Regis Decatur settled in to wait, his rifle snugged up to his shoulder. He was barely able to suppress his giggling fit as he lay there waiting for the killing guns to shout their message of death.

Morgan stood beside the ancient pine tree. After the rain ice had formed on the boughs of the tree and it creaked and groaned now as it shifted heavily in the wind.

Shell listened but he could hear nothing, no careless chatter, no horses shifting their feet. Below the plain stretching out toward the south was empty and dark. The mountains were bleak, serrated silhouettes against the star bright sky.

He heard nothing, but he seemed to sense it, and now his head lifted, his body tensed slightly. He knew they were there, knew it in the marrow of his bones.

Minutes later—hours later?—he heard the creaking of a wagon as it struggled up the long grade behind an eight-horse team. There wasn't as much grease on those axles as there might have been. The horses' hoofs seemed to come down heavily in the night, shaking the earth.

Morgan drew back the hammer of his Winchester and he knew that he wasn't the only man in that darkness to do so.

He stiffened and took the rifle to his shoulder. A lone horseman had appeared on the trail below them, riding in the direction of Hogan.

The wagon came around the bend in the mountain road just as the rider halted his horse and lifted a hand. The wagon braked to a squealing stop.

"Get out of the road, mister, before I blow you off it," the driver of the wagon said. Morgan could see the outriders slow up now, hear cocking of weapons. He wiped the cold sweat from his own forehead and peered down more intently at the ribbon of road below.

"Why, what in the hell's the matter with you hombres?" the man on the horse asked pleasantly. "Think I come to stick you up or something?"

"That could be, my friend. Why don't you just get on off that road and let us by."

"I surely will, I surely will," the lone rider said. Shell identified the soft Virginia accent now. He could see nothing of the man but the vague outline which could have belonged to anyone. "I didn't expect to meet nobody on this trail, gentlemen, pardon me if I'm in the way of something."

"I said get off the road! You're in the way all right, stranger."

"Fine. All right. Don't get touchy," the lone rider said in response. "Let me find a place to get off. I'm not riding a perfectly good horse into that canyon for your pleasure. Think you own the road, do you?"

"See anything. Lou?" the driver asked nervously. He was having trouble holding back the spirited wagon team.

"Nobody. You, Frank?"

"Nothin', but I don't like it. Let's get the hell up the grade and on over."

The lone rider had backed his horse and he now sat the animal in a small hollow just off the road, relaxed and casual, disinterested.

"Please pass, gentlemen," he said.

"You bet we will, damn your eyes," the driver said. He stood up in the box, cracked the long whip he carried above the ears of his team and took the bullet square in the middle of his heart. Then the night split itself open with fire and tumult, the sounds of the guns and the cries of the dying.

9.

Someone had opened the ball and the music was the drum rolls of hell, the dance the jerking reel of death. Shelter saw the driver of the wagon stand up, saw him lift his whip, and then he was blown back out of the box, the shattering roll of the rifle report echoing down the long hills a split second later.

Simultaneously the lone rider on the trail below opened up with a scattergun, blasting two of the outriders from their saddles in a wash of flame and buckshot.

From the north end of the trail, a rebel yell sounded and second later dozens of dark horsemen were pounding down the trail toward the crippled wagon.

Still there was no answering fire from the woods as the vigilantes lay waiting, waiting for the night riders to ride into the teeth of the trap, to fill their gunsights with their bodies.

The outriders escorting the wagon had been mowed

down—they never had a chance, as Decatur had known they wouldn't. The wagon driver and the outriders didn't seem to have known this was a trap, that there was no gold in that wagon, that they were used for bait, that they were quite expendable.

They fought back briefly, but the approaching riders gunned them down and trampled over their bodies, racing toward the wagon and its golden lure.

"Now!" someone, it must have been Decatur, bellowed and the rain of hellfire began. The guns from the trees boomed out their damning message and nightriders fell from their saddles, their horses rearing up, whinnying with pain. Red streaks arrowed out toward the men below and were answered by muzzle flashes, blinking, blinding, deadly eyes, and by the roar of the guns, close and thunderous.

Shelter picked out a near target and shot the night rider through the chest. The man was blown back off the dark figure of his horse, and was dragged away, his boot caught in the stirrup.

The nightriders tried first to ride out of the trap, but there was nowhere to go. Decatur's men controlled both ends of the trail, the high ground as well. Below was sheer precipice and the night riders knew it was fight or die.

They rode their horses straight upslope, a regular cavalry charge in the dead of night with the guns blazing. Shelter felt a bullet impact into the fallen log before him, felt the sting of splinters. They he saw the rider spurring his horse wildly, two guns booming in his hands, and by a flash of gunfire Morgan saw the silver of the spurs, the silver of the Colt revolver, the silver of the holster and belt.

"Cornelius!" he roared, but he couldn't have been heard six feet away with the constant bluster of the war guns.

Shell came up with his rifle, steadied on one knee, snuggled up to the stock of the Winchester and squeezed off. A second too late. The rider turned his horse in answer to a challenge from behind and Morgan held back his fire, not wanting to miss, wanting more than anything in this world to finish this bitter job on this cold and clamorous night.

The horseman turned again, a black silhouette against a blue-black, star spangled sky. Shell took aim, followed the rider with his front bead sight and then hit the deck sharply, suddenly.

The bullet had sung past his ear, passing within inches of his skull.

"Behind you, damnit," Shelter hissed at himself, rolling to the far side of the log as a second bullet pursued him. His injured shoulder flared up with angry pain as he landed. A second shot and a third ticked off the log and Shelter ducked low, cursing as he saw the horseman with the silver-mounted gun vanish into the shadows.

Behind him guns flashed from the dark forest but Morgan couldn't return the fire that was directed at him. He couldn't make out which was friendly fire, which the sniper.

"Someone from the night riders' camp behind us?" He pondered that. "No. Not likely." It had to be someone who wanted him in particular, and there were several good choices for who that might be.

Morgan started to move and yet another slug chipped the log beside his head. Only that time there was a difference. That time he saw the muzzle flash, that time he had spotted his man.

High on the rocks above and behind him, shooting through the pines. Morgan fired twice in return and made his move, darting toward the pines, weaving as he ran, the rifle above flashing two, three more times, the sounds inaudible above the general confusion.

And it was a battlefield across which Shelter ran, there was no doubt of it. He had seen worse, but not at night, not with every man a potential enemy.

There wasn't much to differentiate by. Every man on a horse was assumed to be a night rider, every one afoot, a vigilante. That was all there was to go by. Many of the vigilantes seemed to be firing out of fear, out of the need for self-preservation. Morgan recognized that kind of shooting—pumping as many bullets as possible through your gun in the least amount of time, shooting at anyone who wasn't you. It caused a hell of a lot of wrong-side casualties.

The horseman broke free of the trees, the horse and man bulking large above Morgan who threw himself to one side as the mounted gunman's pistols spoke. Flaming tongues lashed out at Morgan. A face was weirdly lighted momentarily. A face Shell had never seen before, would never see again.

Morgan came up and his own Colt spoke with savage authority. The man was lifted from the saddle to thump to the ground and be trampled by his own panicked horse.

Shelter didn't see the end of it. He fired, knew he had hit, and kept moving, clambering up through the rocks as the gunbattle below swelled to a crescendo of arms, the night coming alive with blistering sound and the roar of the savage guns.

Morgan's eyes were on the rocks, the dark pines, the jagged ridge above him standing stark against the starry sky. There was someone up there who wanted him personally. He couldn't have him.

The rifle spoke again as Morgan got careless and lifted his head a trifle too far. Pulling back, tortoise-like, Shell grimaced and went on. His shoulder was bleeding again, Jean Waltham's stitching and bandaging aside, and it ached like bloody hell. The coldness of the night didn't help. Morgan had shed his coat for ease of movement and now he almost wished he hadn't.

The rifle cracked again and a bullet ricocheted angrily off into the night. Whoever it was up there was getting panicky. That shot wasn't even close.

"He's got the right," Morgan thought. The right to get scared. There was no quick way off that stack of rocks. No way up behind. Which would have made no difference if he had gotten Morgan as he planned. The blame could be passed to the night riders and life could roll merrily on for the sniper.

But he had missed and now he had a bobcat in a barrel.

What he had was Shelter Morgan wounded and angry, armed and ready. The sniper, whoever he was, would have been better off staying home.

The guns still sounded below, but the firing was more sporadic now, more distant. Some of the night riders had broken out on the northern flank and were riding hell bent for home, wherever home happened to be. They had the man with the silver Colt with them, Shell knew, for he hadn't taken his eyes off the man until he could no longer make him out through the darkness and the forest. He had been going north then and there weren't many guns left up that way to stop him.

"I would have had him but for you," Morgan said, looking upslope again, then clinging to the rocks as the rifle fired once more.

Shelter wanted him, wanted him badly. Whoever it was that was shooting there was a good chance that he was the traitor, the inside man for the night riders. If that was so, he knew where the night riders' camp was. He knew where the man with the silver Colt was. Morgan wanted him all right, he wanted him alive and talking.

Shell eased around a massive upthrust tomb-shaped boulder, clinging to the weather cracks in the gray granite. Below there seemed to be only mop-up fire as along the eastern horizon the slow golden moon peered up at the carnage.

The rifle fired again—this time he was seeing ghosts apparently. The shot was ninety degrees away from Morgan's position.

"He's blind," Shell thought and he made the most of it, going up and over the rocks, ignoring the numbing cold, the granite-scoured fingers, the knees knocked painfully against solid stone. The rifleman had lost him and now was the time to move.

Shell leaped up to a narrow ledge, rolled onto his belly and stopped dead. There he was!

Prone, sighting along the barrel of a spanking new Winchester. It might have been the Preacher or the old man himself. It might have been the traitor Morgan was looking for.

It wasn't. It was the kid. Regis Decatur who came around with wide, horror-filled eyes as he saw the tall, bearded man come up out of the rocks, the Colt in his hand, cocked and levelled.

"Drop it, Decatur."

"The hell with you. If I put it down, you'll kill me."

"If you don't, I sure hell will," Morgan growled. "Put it down now."

There was a moment's hesitation and then the rifle hit the deck, ringing on the stone. Regis Decatur raised his hands, his lips curled back in a sneer, his eyes vacillating between fear and challenge. The kid had a problem—maybe his old man loomed too big in his eyes and he was out to prove something, Morgan didn't know.

He only knew he didn't take kindly to being shot at.

"So you're the one, are you?" Morgan asked, moving forward. The moon glowed very brightly now, like a lamp of gold with the wick turned up.

"The one what?" the kid asked sharply, but Morgan could see the fear now, deep in his eyes. There was a trembling in the kid's knees which wasn't from the awesome cold.

"The traitor, the night riders' man."

"Sure," the kid said, laughing out loud. "That's me, all right."

"Why else? Why else do you want to kill me?" Morgan asked. He stopped three paces from the kid. They stood facing each other atop the stack of boulder. Below the firing had stopped. The moon climbed higher, a flattened golden globe.

"Why?" The kid seemed genuinely amazed. "You done me wrong, Marshal Forsberg—whatever your name is."

"Why do you say that?"

"Why? Dad knows you're no marshal. So do I. Who are you then?"

"Your father sent you up here," Shell said, ignoring the question. *Daltry, damnit, I never should have slipped there.* "Well, answer me!"

"Hell, no, he didn't send me. He wouldn't trust me to do a job like this anyway. I told you," the kid said almost frantically. "I did this on my own. You done me wrong, Forsberg. You showed me up in front of . . . damn! No!" The scream that issued from the kid's lips was smothered by the racketing gunshot.

Morgan spun, dropped to his belly and rolled, catching only a brief glimpse of the kid going down, his chest smudged with blood, his shirt front lifting as a second bullet tagged home. Shelter saw that, saw the gunman shift his sights, saw the Preacher white and calm and deadly squeeze off again and then he was rolling down the pile of rocks, fresh pain tearing at his shoulder, a stone cracking his skull, the distant roaring echo of gunfire filling his ears until he landed with a solid thunk against a stone ledge far, far below and the moon swam past in the inky sky, a grinning, pale moon with the narrow, mocking features of the Preacher.

". . . the bastard."

". . . colder than shit too."

"Shut up. For a thousand dollars I'd . . ."

The voices came from a vast distance. The wind bent the words, rearranged them, distorted their meaning. But there was no wind blowing. There was only the storm twisting and foaming through Shelter Morgan's brain. His head began to ache now, to ache horribly and he remembered falling from the rocks, remembered the blazing guns of the Preacher as he shot into the body of Regis Decatur, as he tried to kill Morgan.

"I don't get it," a voice, disembodied, rasping said, "was he a marshal or wasn't he? I ain't gonna kill no lawman and I don't care who gives the order or what the price on his head is."

"He's no lawman," someone answered.

Shelter started as he realized that the dark shape he saw pasted against the sky was a man's shoulders and head, that he was standing hunched not fifteen feet from here Morgan lay cramped and twisted between the rocks surrounding him. He switched his eyes for one second, looking up. He had fallen a long way, cracked his head and gone out. The Preacher then must have come looking—or maybe he had been interrupted—but no one had found Morgan. They must have thought he had gotten out of the area if they hadn't found him by now.

"Who the hell is he then?"

"One of them. One of the night riders."

"I knew he was a Reb, but how could he be a night rider spy? He only showed up tonight."

"He was just a new wrinkle, Ed, don't you see anything? Weren't you listenin' to Decatur? Look at this—with a US marshal standing around, how are we going to get our work done? He's going to object to everything, or maybe lead us off the trail dead into their sights. It would have worked neat except he screwed it up."

Yes, Morgan thought, I did screw it up. Damn it all to hell. He tried to move his hand toward his holstered Colt and discovered two things—that hand would not move properly and there was no gun in his holster. He must have lost it falling.

The gun didn't worry him so much as the hand. That scared him silly.

"Then Bill Waltham was in with him?"

"Sure, hell yes, must've been. Bill brought him in, didn't he? Besides, Waltham's a Reb too. Arkansawyer. Decatur will take care of Waltham too, right and proper."

"Hang him?"

"What do you think?" the answering voice sneered. "Regis is dead, ain't he? This Marshal Forsberg, whoever the hell he is, killed him, didn't he? And who brought Forsberg in—why, Bill Waltham. What the hell do you think the old man's going to do about it?"

There was a nasty little laugh following that and the hunters moved away, leaving their wounded quarry in the rocks.

"Damnit, Bill, I'm sorry." The kid hadn't wanted anything much to do with Morgan, hadn't wanted to take him in, to escort him to Decatur's house, but he had, maybe out of a sense of justice or fair play. Jean had urged him to do it, but it had been Bill's decision in the end, and if he had wanted to he could have refused. And now for his help he was going to be hung.

Shelter started to rise again, but it was hard as hell. The right arm didn't want to do anything, the left was bleeding, his head rang and his guts were churning. It was almost a relief when the search party again passed the rocks where he lay and he had to settle back unmoving, watching the moon float past overhead.

He went out again, somehow slept or just plain passed out. When he awoke it was the dead of night, all of the world had gone to icy blackness.

Shelter slowly lifted his aching head, hearing nothing, seeing nothing.

Yet they couldn't have gone, not all of them. Even if they believed by now that he must have made his escape, there would be a man or two left behind to cover this contingency.

The trouble was, Morgan just wasn't prepared to handle them. He couldn't fight and he knew it; he couldn't run and he couldn't stay where he was.

That didn't leave a hell of a lot of choices—outside of lying down to die.

Morgan wasn't preapred to do that. He clawed at the ice-slicked rocks beside him and gradually lifted himself to a sitting position. He sat there fighting back the waves of nausea, the starbursts behind his eyes, the whirring confusion of his brain.

His teeth had begun to chatter and he couldn't remember for a time why he had thrown his coat away. Then he did and he cursed himself.

A voice. Was that a voice, or the wind creaking in the trees? The moaning of the ghosts of the dead. Yeah, there were numbers of dead now. The forest still rang with the shots, with their screams. And Sherman would be coming . . . Morgan shook his head. This wasn't Georgia and *that* war was long over.

His thoughts were confused and he wanted to lie down and sleep, but if he did that, he thought, he would die. They would find him and he would die. Besides, Morgan didn't like unconsciousness, he could barely tolerate sleep. He didn't like being drunk, losing time, losing contact with his body, drifting away . . . yes, that was a voice that time.

To his left and through the woods. Two men now, talking in low voices. Apparently they too believed that Morgan had made his escape and that they were only following orders to keep Lewis Decatur happy.

Shelter gripped the rock beside him and rose up like a dead man rising from the grave. He finally got to his feet and staggered into motion, placing one foot in front of the other as he moved toward the voices. He didn't want to go that way—his instinct was to turn and run, to hobble up into the mountains, but those men had things he needed.

A gun, a horse, information.

Where was Bill Waltham? Hanging from a tree in the pine forest? If not, Morgan owed him, owed his sister. Those men would know that.

Morgan stopped, his head swimming. He had to be dreaming—there was a fire blazing in the clearing, pine-scented smoke rising through the dark trees, two men sitting close to the fire.

He had to be dreaming—they couldn't be such fools. But they were cold and the night was long and their vigil was a lonely one. They had every reason to believe that Shelter Morgan was long gone, that the mountains were safe on that dark night.

They were wrong, dead wrong.

The night was only just beginning and what had been a very cold and empty forest was suddenly to be filled with hot blood and blind panic.

10.

The thing crouched at the perimeter of the circle of dull reddish light cast by the fire. The thing which was not at this moment quite human because the two men who sat by the fire, warm and snug, were armed and waited only to kill it.

To kill Shelter Morgan, and he wouldn't have it. It wasn't personal at all, but neither was the killing of a rattler or a black widow spider. It was simply a matter of killing so that you might survive, and ethics flew out the window.

The night was cold. Shelter's teeth chattered. He had no good plan, no plan at all. They had the guns, they had the coats, the warm, warm coats, their horses near the fire. He had a savage need to survive.

"Howdy, men."

He walked right up to them. Both of them were squatting beside the fire, one near Shell, one across the fire ring.

"Got any coffee?"

"Why, damn you, it's . . ." the man started to come to his feet, but he was too slow. Morgan was a big cat mauling him, his bowie plucked from the sheath at the back of his belt doing its deadly work. As the vigilante clawed at his sidearm, trying to bring it to bear, Morgan's bowie flashed in the firelight, ripping up, striking the jugular, tearing it wide as the man grappled with Shell, trying to kill before he could be killed.

The Colt was in his hand and then it was in Shell's and Morgan was firing across the body of the dying man, his bullets lifting the second vigilante to his toes as the shotgun the Decatur man carried emptied itself into the earth, scattering dirt and flame, firewood and ashes as the double-ten spat out its load of smoking lead.

"Ed!" From the forest another voice called out and Shelter backed away, his dark hair hanging in his eyes, the captured Colt in his hand. He bent down and started unbuttoning the buffalo coat the blood-stained vigilante at his feet wore.

"Ed? Carl? What the hell's going on?"

The horses, Morgan noted with dismay, had jerked free of their tethers and were long gone, galloping free through the woods.

"Ed? Holy Jesus!" The rifleman cut loose and Shelter, firing back off-handedly with the Colt as he ran, made for the deeper pines, searching bullets pinging and whining off the trees near him.

Not two men, not three, but a half dozen had been left behind to watch for Morgan when Decatur pulled off. He could hear them now hurriedly organizing themselves, getting their horses, shouting instructions—and Morgan was alone and afoot. Time to get the hell out of there and he started off at a hobbling run.

He needed a horse—Shell pulled the buffalo coat on

106

and buttoned it up—a horse and more ammunition, time to organize his thoughts, to plan out . . . two riders came slowly through the pines and Morgan dropped to the ground to lie there against the cold earth as they rode past.

A horse . . . the Waltham place. How far was that? He didn't think it was more than a mile or two up over the sharp sawtoothed ridge above him. If he could get there and get warm, find a horse and a box of .44s . . . what then?

There wasn't any point of thinking about "what then," the thing to do was to move, to keep moving. Shelter started toward the serrated ridge above him. The moon painted the earth silver where water seeped from the rocks.

What about Bill Waltham? Hung? Tortured? And Jean? They would likely think the girl was involved in this as well, being Bill's sister. The vigilantes were seeing night riders everywhere.

Again from behind Shelter horses appeared. The riders might have seen him, but they didn't. For once luck was with him on this night and as he went to the ground again they rode past. Maybe, he thought, they don't want to see me, to see anything. Maybe they're intelligent men and long for nothing more than a warm bed, a warm meal, a warm and loving woman on this night.

When they were gone Shelter got to his feet again and began climbing the ridge. There was no way up the slope for a horse and as the road fell away, the forest thinning, Morgan began to feel looser, to grow confident.

"Confident," he thought almost laughing out loud. "That's a damned funny word for it." He had ridden in yesterday unknown, a harmless stranger. Tonight he was being hunted by the vigilantes of Hogan, hunted by the night riders. He had blown this one, blown it completely. Half of the territory was looking for him, ready and quite eager to stretch his neck or shoot him so full of lead that he would do for a clipper ship's anchor.

Morgan was nearly to the crest of the ridge. The moon was bright, silver, round. His shadow snaked across the rocks as he climbed. Behind all was silent as only the dead can be silent.

He made the peak of the sawtoothed ridge and sat down, gasping for breath, his pulse throbbing through his injured shoulder. His right arm was all right now—apparently lying as he had for hours on end had just shut off the blood supply, numbing it. But his head was aching something fierce. He didn't want to touch it, to find out if it was split open, cracked or just caved in.

He sat there breathing deeply, each breath bringing a new wave of pain. Above him the moon shone brightly. He couldn't see Hogan from there, but only the vast bald head of Big Dome. There was no light where he thought the Sky Ridge Ranch should be, but then maybe there was no one there who could light a lamp.

"Would they hurt her?" he asked himself. The answer was, yeah, they would hurt Jean Waltham if they thought she knew something, if they thought they could get it out of her, if they thought she and her brother were hooked in with the night riders somehow.

"Touch her, Decatur," Morgan swore to the dark and empty land, "and you're a dead man. I promise you that. Touch a hair of her head and you are going to regret it through eternity."

He started off down the long sloping ridge, his teeth chattering, his head aching. The old shoulder wound had stiffened up but he was aware of that only in a distant way. Closer to the arena of consciousness was the ache of bruised ribs, the hammering of blood in his skull.

He was a hunted man now, hunted by every two-legged man in the mountains. Decatur would have his men out looking. At the Waltham's? Sure, why not—still Morgan had to try for the house. There was nowhere else to go. He needed a horse badly, very badly . . .

He stumbled and went down, pitching head first down the icy, rocky slope before him. When he dragged himself to his feet again the moon had shifted, the night had grown colder yet. There was hoarfrost on his beard. His fingers were cramped and numb.

Morgan thought at first that the light he saw ahead of him through the dark trees was a product of the blow on the head. But the longer he focused on it, the more real it became. A light—from where? It had to be the Waltham cabin by his reckoning and he scrambled to his feet to trudge on across the broken slabs of black shale as the moon beat down, glossing the weird icy landscape before him.

The Waltham cabin. He reached it an hour later and still later he went to his belly to lie looking down at it from the piny ridge.

There was a lamp in the front window—he didn't know if that was normal or not. Maybe she left a light there for Bill on nights he was out. It painted a pale rectangle on the damp, frosted ground outside. Shelter tried to focus on the yard, to tell if horses had trampled up the earth, but it was impossible at that distance.

He had to get down there, had to, and so he started slithering through the pines, moving on his belly, his every sense sharpened incredibly. The house was still, the trees around him stood together in dark, motionless masses. The moon was a search beacon staring down at the cold dark world.

Morgan was within a hundred feet of the house now, lying on his belly behind a ridge which had had the young trees trimmed from it. Their narrow stumps dotted the hillside. Thirty feet in front of him there was an old outbuilding, of stone. It appeared to be older than the house itself. Its use was uncertain, but its windowless design made Shell think it must have once been a smokehouse.

Beyond the smokehouse was another twenty to thirty feet of open ground then the rough pole and sod stable, then twenty more feet to the house.

If he stayed where he was all night they would find him stiff and cold in the morning—if the dead could be any colder than he was at that moment.

He had to move. He took the bowie from the back of his belt and started forward, gathering himself into a crouch before launching himself into a careening, staggering run toward the smokehouse.

He pressed up against the wall of the stone building, hearing birds or rodents in the ceiling. Peering around the corner of the building he saw nothing else. Gathering himself again he started toward the stable. Reaching it he found Jean's horse there and the big bay the marshal had been riding. They eyed him with some suspicion until he rested a hand on the shoulder of each briefly. He squatted there, between the horses, feeling the warmth of their bodies, watching the back of the house.

Then he started on—maybe they hadn't yet thought of sending a man to the Waltham house. That didn't mean they wouldn't come riding up, a dozen strong, at any minute. Shelter had killed the big man's son—or they thought he had. Only the Preacher knew the truth of things. If he could find him, now . . . but he wasn't going to find the Preacher on the Sky Ridge Ranch.

Shelter was at the back door of the house and he stretched out a hand. The latch string was out and he gripped the rawhide gingerly, slowly tugging until he heard the bar slide. Then, sucking it up, Shelter Morgan stepped into the dark interior of cabin.

The wash of flame and sound stung the night. Shelter had gone in low and rolling, not trusting to appearances, and the bullet flew past over his head, splintering the wood of the doorframe. By the muzzle flash Shelter had seen his man.

Across the room, three strides? Four. Four would be too many. Morgan sprang toward the ambusher, hearing the lever action being worked on the Winchester he faced. Two strides, three, and Morgan slashed out with the bowie as a second shot rang loudly in the close confines of the cabin, as the acrid black powder smoke clogged the room. Morgan's knife blade struck flesh.

He had hit the vigilante high on the chest, penetrated through the sternum and struck heart muscle with the tip of the bowie. A gurgling cry rose from the throat of the vigilante. The rifle clattered to the stone floor.

Morgan could feel the man writhing on the point of his knife, feel the steady gush of hot blood pumping from the wounded man's body, feel the panicked, frantic blows the vigilante aimed blindly at Morgan.

Then there was nothing else. The man went still and slack. He collapsed to the floor, taking Shelter with him.

Morgan landed roughly, slamming the injured shoulder into the floor. Waves of jarring, flaming agony swept through him but he fought it off. It subsided in slow tidal pulsings finally and he got to hands and knees, yanking the knife from the vigilante's chest, searching for the rifle.

He found the Winchester and looked to the inner door. Where was Jean? If she was not bound up or hurt, she would have been there by now. If she was hurt, or dead, every vigilante in that army of Decatur's would feel the sting of Morgan's retribution. Yet he doubted they would hurt her for one reason—there was just no point in it. She had nothing they wanted; she couldn't even have known where Morgan was.

Tied up then, bound and gagged? Likely, and likely in the next room which was the living room. Shelter put the Winchester down, leaning it against the wall beside the door. Then silently, quickly he crossed to where the dead man lay.

He was heavy, all dead weight is heavy beyond logic, beyond the rules of physics. He got the man before him and braced him against the door. Then, reaching around to pick up the rifle, Shell opened the door.

The hinges shrilled loudly and the dead man fell into the room. And the guns from behind the sofa opened up, riddling the corpse with bullets. Shelter saw it jerk and jump as the bullets plowed through it, digging up the floor beneath, he saw that and simultaneously saw the girl tied in a chair across the room, her head bowed, her hair snarled.

Shelter brought the rifle to his shoulder and fired four times. Left, right, high, low, through the back of the sofa and a piercing scream filled the cabin. A man leaped to his feet and started back-pedalling away, his hands waving in frantic circles. Blood smeared his throat and chest. He slammed into the stone fireplace and went down. The second one lay behind the sofa whining with pain. The bullet had taken him in the groin and there was a smear of blood where his manhood should have been.

"Finish me," the man begged as Morgan came around the sofa to stand over him, looking down into a pain contorted face. "Finish the job. It hurts, God, it hurts!"

He didn't have to finish the job. The man stiffened and his eyes went wide. Then he slumped back and the hurting was over. Forever.

112

Jean's eyes were wide and worried. Morgan was to her in three long steps, untying the gag first.

"Are there any more of them?" was the first question he wanted answered.

"No. There were three. Just three. Bill . . ."

"Bill's all right. He's alive anyway."

"But things didn't go well, did they?" Jean asked. Shell's eyes met hers as his bowie prepared to slice away the ropes that tied her to the stiff-backed wooden chair.

"They didn't go right, no. They got onto me somehow—my own fault, I guess. Then Regis Decatur was killed. They have the idea I did it. They've got Bill, I guess, and they'll be blaming him for taking me down there."

"My God, they'll lynch him."

"Not if I can help it," Morgan said.

Jean leaped up out of her chair, but the circulation had been cut off for a while and her body betrayed her. She staggered and Shelter had to catch her.

"What do you mean they got onto you, marshal?" she asked, and those blue eyes were shrewd now, shrewd and accusing.

"I'm no marshal, Jean."

"Oh, God! I was right all along." She tried to pull away from Shelter, but he held her tightly.

"You weren't right then and you're not right now. I'm not an enemy of yours, listen to me, damnit! Turn your head and look at me. Listen! I'm on your side, girl. I'm going to try and get Bill from them if I can. I'm here in the mountains because of some business of my own, business I don't care to talk about right now. There's not time to discuss it anyway. But, a man apparently has to choose sides in these mountains—all right, I'm with you. Do you understand?"

"No," Jean said and her voice was chilly, "I don't understand a bit. What is your business here? Why did

113

you pretend you were a marshal? Why did you go along tonight, put yourself in front of the guns if you don't have a stake in the war between the vigilantes and the night riders?"

"Jean, I can't tell you now. Not now. Get a coat, and some food, a blanket or two."

"For what? I'm not leaving."

"You'll have to leave. They'll be back, won't they?"

"Back? What for? You're going?"

Shelter looked at the woman closely. Her eyes were glazed, her thoughts didn't seem to be quite organized. "Get yourself a shot of whisky," he told her. "It's cold out and you'll need it. I'm moving you because I want you safe when I go after Bill—understand me?"

"Where can I go?" Jean asked. She stepped back and just stood looking at Morgan, arms hanging limply. "I can't leave the ranch! They'll rob us blind. There won't be a steer left on the place in twenty-four hours."

"Maybe not, but they're not worth dying for. They just aren't. Do what I've told you now, we're getting out."

Getting out and taking her where? He had only one idea. He wanted a strong man who couldn't be intimidated, a man with guns around. Preferably one who had a woman living with him.

Only Sailor Logan fit the bill so far as Shelter knew. Whether Logan would do it or not, Morgan didn't know, but he had the idea that when Logan gave his word a thing was done. He stood up to the night riders with only his young son and daughter behind him. He stood up to his detractors at the vigilante meeting and he stood up to Morgan. Likely he would stand again.

"I'm ready," Jean said. She had a hat and scratched leather jacket on. She carried a blanket roll and a sack of supplies. She looked very small, childlike. Shell crossed the room to her and kissed her softly on her pale lips. She didn't complain, didn't respond.

"Let's ride then, woman. This is going to be a long night." A long one and a bloody one. They went out into the darkness and began drifting toward the hell that lay ahead of them.

The wind was blowing hard off of the mountains. The trail wound through the hills, the pines crowding around them. Dropping down into a hollow Jean pulled her horse up sharply and Shelter frowned.

"What is it?"

"Get down."

"What's the trouble, Jean?"

"Please," she said and there was something in her starlit eyes which caused Morgan to comply.

He swung down and dropped the reins to his horse and she walked to him, kissing him deeply.

"We haven't got the time to fool around, woman," Morgan said, holding her at arms' length.

"Who's fooling?" she answered. "I've wanted you since I first saw you. Now I'm standing right at the edge of losing you without ever having had you, and I just can't take it—do you understand!" The tears had begun to fill her eyes and Shelter kissed her softly, tasting them as they trickled down her face. It was foolish maybe, but he wanted her as much as she wanted him. Walking close to death can make the need grow stronger sometimes. It had happened to Jean; it was happening to Morgan.

"My bedroll," she said breathlessly, and in seconds Shell had it untied and spread on the ground back among the great pines which swayed and creaked in the wind. It was cold as Morgan stepped from his clothes, warm in the hastily made bed where the soft and anxious woman lay, her arms reaching out for him, her eyes starlit, her hair loose, spread across the blanket.

Morgan was in beside her in seconds and she wrapped him in her arms, drawing him down to her hungrily searching mouth. "Don't fool around," she said. "Don't wait. I don't want to wait."

He didn't make her wait. His need was as urgent as Jean's on this windy, dark night, and alone with her on that wilderness slope he was as primitive and timeless as the forest. He slipped his hands beneath her softly molded ass and lifted her, positioning her. Her fingers groped for his shaft, finding it, easing him into her soft warmth as her hips began to way and pitch, as her down-cushioned pelvis began to tap rhythmically against Morgan's.

She put her hands behind his head and dragged him down to her breasts and he tasted them lingeringly, his tongue toying with the taut buds as Jean's breathing began to grow ragged and harsh, as she groped for him, touching his shaft where he entered her, feeling the slow slip and sway of him.

"It's good," she breathed into his ear, "very good."

Her mouth found his, her breath was warm and moist, her body attacking his, driving against him, enveloping him with heat and need, clutching, probing until she came with a gasp of surprise, a deep purr of pleasure and Shelter's own hard climax followed, sudden, satisfying and they lay together in the deep forest, holding on to each other's warmth as the cold night drifted past.

11.

The door opened and the man with the shotgun stood looking into Shelter Morgan's eyes.

"Get ready to die," Sailor Logan said.

He was wearing his trousers, mule-ear boots, underwear shirt and a very nasty expression. The shotgun was level at his hip, those two ten-gauge muzzles looking like railroad tunnels.

"We've got to talk," Morgan said mildly.

"No, we *don't* got to talk, Mr. Whoever-you-are." It was only then that Sailor Logan saw the young woman standing beside her horse, saw her sway and cling to the pommel of her saddle for support. "Miss Waltham?" He looked at Shelter again. "Is she hurt, man?"

"No, just roughed up a little. Decatur's people did it."

"Clara!" Sailor Logan yelled across his shoulder and the girl, carrying a rifle, appeared instantly. She was fifteen or so, red haired, freckled. "Clara, Jean Waltham's here and she's ailing. Get her inside."

The girl, eyeing Shelter with much suspicion, brushed past her father and got Jean. Together the women walked back into the house.

"Harry, you keep your eye on this fellow," Sailor Logan said, and Shelter saw the kid at the front window move.

"Sure will, Pa."

"Talk then," Logan said sourly.

"It might take a minute."

"Talk. Out here."

"All right. First off I didn't kill Regis Decatur. The Preacher did that. For the pure hell of it as far as I could tell. Both of them were trying to kill me, Sailor—what do you think of that?" Shell leaned against the pole which supported the porch awning.

"I don't think nothin' of it, and why should I?" the old salt grumbled.

"No reason. I thought you maybe knew something about why they would want to kill me, that's all."

"I ain't no back shooter and no ambusher."

"No. I know that, that's why I brought the girl here, Sailor," Morgan replied.

"Cause you like me."

"In a manner of speaking. You got two feet to stand on anyway."

"Even if I did set the dogs on you," Sailor said, turning his head but not his eyes to spit.

"Why wouldn't you? You caught me up in a foolish mistake. You knew I wasn't what I said I was."

"That's right," Sailor drawled.

"So I had to be a night rider."

"It figured."

Shelter smiled, "Well, it might have figured, but it was wrong. I'm not with the night riders, never heard of them until I talked to your brother out in California."

"You did talk to Daltry then."

"Sure. He and I go back a way. He told me a little about you and a little about what was going on up here."

"And he gave you some of that good brandy he's always buying," Sailor suggested.

"Sailor, I'm telling this story straight—there's no point in trying to trip me up. Expensive brandy? Your brother thinks a dime for a shot of belly-rotting whisky is too much, and he's seldom got the dime. I know—I did the buying the whole time we were together."

"Yeah," Sailor chuckled. "I always did too. I'm starting to believe you just a little, my friend. A little because whatever my brother is, Daltry Logan is no whisky fool—he don't tell everything he knows for the price of a drink. Leastwise, he never did before. And he wouldn't be sending a stranger to my place if he didn't trust him somewhat."

"All right—you believe me a little, that's enough. All I want from you, Sailor, is for you to take care of that girl for a time. I trust *you* for that."

"And what are you going to do, meanwhile?"

"Meanwhile I'm going to get Bill Waltham from Decatur—he doesn't deserve to die for what happened."

"No, he don't," Logan said. "These are bad times, mister, people want to kill to solve all their problems. Some of us are just wrapped up in all of this so tightly we can't turn away from it. It's a killing time and a bad thing it is."

"It's a bad time," Shelter agreed.

"You never did get around to telling me what brought you to these mountains," Logan said shrewdly.

"No? It's a man, Sailor Logan, a man I'm looking for."

"Is that so? It's a killing grudge?"

"It is that, Sailor Logan, it is that."

"Then I'm glad I ain't the man—or am I?"

"No, Sailor, you're not. We wouldn't be talking if you were."

"No. I guess we wouldn't. Goodbye then, mister. Goodbye, and don't hurry back. I wasn't glad to see you tonight; I don't care if I ever see you again." Sailor paused. "The girl, she'll be all right. Don't you fret about that. And tell Bill to come by if he can. I'll set them both on the right trail to somewhere if I can."

"Thanks, Sailor."

Logan snorted in disdain. "Don't thank me for what's only right and decent, mister. There's still some in these mountains that know what common courtesy and human kindness might be."

Then Sailor stepped backward and the door to his sturdy house banged shut uncompromisingly. Shelter smiled slowly, walked to the marshal's big bay horse and swung up, sparing a last glance at the window where two rifles were still trained on him, before— lifting his hat in farewell—he turned the horse and started toward Hogan once again. Hogan and the vigilante boss. Hogan and the guns of night.

The tap at the door brought the big man's head up. He was slumped in the red leather chair, a brandy glass in his scarred white hand.

"Yeah?" Lewis Decatur called from out of the blur of sleep and liquor.

"It's me, sir." Frank Hutchins came in, his big-shouldered body filling the entire frame of the doorway. He was massive and dependable, was Frank. Eight years a mine foreman for Decatur in various parts of Colorado. A head-buster when he had to be, utterly faithful. Just now the sight of him angered Decatur.

"What the hell is it?"

"He won't talk."

"He won't talk!" Decatur mimicked. "A pantywaist like that? A kid? You can't get him to talk, Frank? Do I have to show you how to do it?"

"He's tougher than he looks, sir. Surprising tough." Hutchins said defensively.

Decatur had lifted himself to his feet. Now he crossed the room and poured himself another glass of brandy. He tossed it down, hardly tasting it.

"It's not that I loved the kid, Frank, you understand that?" Hutchins nodded. Decatur was standing in front of a gold-framed mirror, imported from Florence, Italy. He could see his mine foreman's big head bob up and down, see the dull-witted mind working on the thought.

"I get you, Mister Decatur," Frank said, though he obviously didn't.

"It's not that I loved him," Decatur went on. "He was a sick one, was Regis. Sick, distorted. As his sister is. Did you know Gloria is distorted, Frank?"

"She's right beautiful, sir," Frank Hutchins said in some confusion.

"Sick. Both of them. The little bastard was no good, but damn them, Frank!" The hand holding the glass slammed down against the sideboard and the room rumbled with his voice. Glass met glass somewhere and it broke, leaving Decatur's hand bloodied. He paid no attention to it. "They can't do this to me or to mine! They can't take what is *mine* and destroy it. I won't be robbed or insulted or injured."

"No, sir."

"Frank—do you understand what I'm telling you? Make the kid talk, Frank. When they killed Regis they robbed me of something the same as they rob me when they take my gold. Maybe he wasn't much, but he was mine! I want the man who did it."

"I'll try again, sir."

"You do that, Frank. You do that. Who's with him now?"

"Just Andy. Andy and me, boss."

"I thought maybe the Preacher—"

"No, sir, he's gone to bed. You know him, he ain't so good at certain things."

"No." No, he wasn't. The pale, silent man was good at practically nothing but gunplay. But he was good at that. Oh, yes, he was good with that black little mamba of a Colt he carried.

"Wait." Decatur held up a hand, noticed it was bloody and sucked at it. "I'm going with you, Frank. I want to talk to him myself."

The two men went out into the carpeted hall and walked along the balustraded corridor toward the main stairway. The grandfather clock in the lower hall struck three a.m.

"Father?"

Decatur looked toward the room to his right. She stood there in a sheer white gown, a gown that showed every curve of her figure, voluptuous and hungry as the light behind her silhouetted her. Frank looked away in embarrassment.

"What is it, Gloria?"

"I thought I heard something."

"Me. You heard me, dear. Go to bed now."

"Yes. I just thought I heard something," she said again, and that distant, crooked smile parted and lifted her full lips. Silently Gloria closed the door.

The two men hurried on. They went down into the cold cellar, the slapping sounds, the muffled groans of pain growing louder as they reached its depths.

"Damn you, who is he!" Andy demanded. His hand fell again, the flat of it striking hard against the bruised and bloodied face of Bill Waltham, turning his head.

There was no answer from Waltham, none at all. He sat looking past his torturer and after a moment Andy realized that Decatur and Frank were there.

"Nothing, Mr. Decatur," Andy said, wiping the perspiration from his head. "Just nothing at all. He's tough as nails—who'd 'ave thought it." He shook his head in wonder, flexing his right hand which was sore and cramped, bruised from banging against the prisoner's head and body. Two solid hours Andy had been at it. Two hours and the kid hadn't cracked an inch.

"Go to the kitchen and get yourself some coffee, Andy," Decatur told him. "I want to talk to Waltham myself."

"Yes, sir, Mr. Decatur." Andy glanced at Frank Hutchins and then ducked past them, going up the stairs, the leather heels of his boots clacking on the planks.

Bill Waltham sat watching the old man, feeling the blood trickle from nostrils and mouth, feeling the loose teeth on the right side where Hutchins had gotten too exuberant. His hands were tied behind him and had no feeling whatsoever in them. He hoped he didn't lose them—that had been known to happen. What was a man to do without hands?

"You little bastard," Decatur said, coming nearer. Without another word, without warning, he kicked Bill Waltham on the shin, just below the knee. The pain was shattering. Bill moaned involuntarily. His mind began playing all sorts of crazy games. Liquid fire rolled through his skull and tiny pirouetting bundles of needles jabbed at the sensitive nerve ending there.

"Who was he?" Decatur demanded, leaning low so that Bill could smell the brandy, the meat scent of his breath. "Who the hell was this Forsberg?"

"Don't know," Bill gasped, and Decatur kicked him again in exactly the same spot. The pain was excruciating.

"Who?" Decatur asked again, and the tone was mild. There was a nasty gleam in his eyes and Bill had the horrible feeling that he had discovered where Regis and Gloria had gotten their madness from. From Dad, from Lewis Decatur who wasn't quite there now.

"I don't know. He told me he was a marshal. He had papers to prove it. I swear to you, that's the way it happened!"

Decatur turned his back to the prisoner. "You didn't know him back home, in Arkansas?"

"No."

"That is home, isn't it?"

"Yes," Bill panted, grateful for the chance to talk again, for any respite from the pain. "Arkansas."

"And you're a merchant down there, or were before your sister sent for you."

"That's right, yes." Frank Hutchins stood behind the old man, huge and menacing, a darkscowl tugging down at his mouth.

"A merchant—what does that mean exactly? What did you deal in?"

"All sorts of commodities. It depended. Molasses, rice, cotton."

"Buying and selling?" Decatur turned again. There was a little smile on his face, a smile that didn't belong there.

"That's right," Bill answered cautiously.

"What's cotton going for by the bale?" Decatur demanded.

"It's . . ." damnit, there was a blank spot in his memory just then. Bill knew, should know, but he couldn't answer just then, couldn't find the information in his mind. "It varies," he said a little desperately.

"Yes, of course. From what to what, would you say?

How much does it vary? What is the average price, would you say? Never mind!" Decatur exploded. "Never mind answering, it's obvious you haven't an idea in the world. It's obvious you're lying, Waltham. Why, Waltham?" He savagely lifted Bill's chin. "Why are you lying to me? These men think you're a tough nut to crack, Waltham. Do you know what—I don't think so at all. I think they haven't gone about it in the proper way. What do you think, Waltham!"

The voice was taunting now, and there was a vast confusion in Waltham's mind. He couldn't dredge up an answer. He just shook his head miserably.

Decatur's huge fist rose again but it hovered over Bill's head, not descending. Slowly it lowered and Decatur became quiet, rational, nearly familiar again.

"Look, Waltham, this can't be easy for you. All I want is the truth, don't you understand? Sure you do. You're a tough man, all right. I admit it. You were in the war, huh? You must have been, a man your age. Confederate? You don't have to be afraid of admitting that to me now. Is that what you were? Is that where you met Forsberg, in the army?"

Bill Waltham stared up at Decatur, his dark eyes bloodshot, his nose still trickling blood, his face gray and bruised.

"I told you about how I met Forsberg—whoever the hell he is! I met him at the ranch. He came there with my sister. I don't know anything else about him."

"You're lying, Waltham."

"Oh, Jesus," Bill said in exasperation.

"That's one talent I'm said to have, and it's done me good service in business—I can tell when a man's lying to me, Waltham, did you know that?"

"You're wrong this time, I'm telling you."

"No." Decatur's voice went soft and low again and Bill Waltham knew that it was coming.

They're going to kill me now, he thought.

Decatur hung over him, his big fists bunched. Behind him Frank Hutchins watched placidly, like a great dumb ox. Decatur's boot toe stretched out and hooked the leg of Bill's chair. He yanked back savagely and the chair upended. Waltham fell over backward and his head rang against the floor. He lay there on his side feeling small and cold and battered. Decatur kicked him in the kidneys, kicked him again and the pain nearly took the top of Bill Waltham's head off.

"That's enough," the quiet, distantly familiar voice said from the stairs. "Kick him again and I'll blow you in half, Decatur."

Decatur spun as did Frank Hutchins. Hutchins made the mistake of grabbing for his holstered Russian pistol and Shelter Morgan shot him through the leg just above the knee. Hutchins screamed and went down on the floor, rolling around, gripping his leg with both hands, trying to stem the flow of blood.

Morgan walked toward him and kicked the gun away. His eyes never left Decatur's face.

"My men will kill you; you'll never get away with this," Decatur said. He took a half step forward in his rage before reason reminded him that he could easily join Frank on the cellar floor.

"There's no one around, Decatur. I made sure of that. There was one man in the kitchen upstairs, but he won't be any trouble now. Outside of that there's no one around. Untie Bill, won't you." Shell's voice was gentle, nearly purring, but there was a tone of command in it, command augmented by the big six shooter and Decatur walked toward the kid, the groans of Frank Hutchins still in his ears.

"That shot will bring them running," Decatur said.

"Untie the ropes." Morgan looked around. "I doubt much sound escapes this room—that's probably why you had it built this way."

Decatur had gotten most of the ropes free, enough for Bill Waltham to stand and face Shelter, his hands still bound behind him, his face lumpy and bruised.

"Thanks," Waltham said. "You take chances, don't you?"

"I've been known to."

"How's . . . ?"

"Jean's fine. She'll be a lot better after she knows that you're all right. Hurry it up, Decatur, damn you."

"You killed my son," Decatur said. Then he said it again, his eyes glowing softly. "You killed Regis."

"Like hell I did. You want to know who killed him, you talk to a pale-haired little man in black."

"The Preacher?"

"That's what I said. He's the one who killed your boy, Decatur, not me."

"You're a god damned liar!" The big man's face was suffused with blood, crimson and ugly. He stood there with the loose coils of rope in his hand, his eyes boring holes in Shelter.

"No," Morgan went on, still quietly. "I'm not lying to you. You're one of those men who can't stand to hear the truth if you don't like it. The Preacher did it. Not me. The kid came gunning for me. Maybe he wanted to impress you, I don't know. He came gunning and I swung around and caught him with his pants down. The Preacher tried to take us both out. He shot the kid first—that was his mistake, he should have tried taking me first."

"Why? I don't believe it. Why would he do that?"

"You'd have to ask the Preacher about that, Decatur. I haven't got the time to stand and discuss it just now. I don't know when your people might be coming around. Just tie this man up, will you?"

Shelter nodded toward Hutchins and stepped back as Decatur tied the mine foreman, very tightly without being told. Morgan waved the gun at him again. "Now step back, will you? Lift up that chair and have a seat. Bill? Can you take care of Mr. Decatur for us?"

"Sure. Sit down, Decatur. Better let me have that rope."

The big man was tied into the chair. His anger hadn't subsided, but there was something else in his expression now—uncertainty. He half-believed Morgan's tale.

"Who are you, Forsberg?" he asked.

"Just a man passing through." Morgan was looking at the wound on Hutchins' leg. The big man was in pain, hard pain. Shell told him, "You'll make it, man, if they find you in the next few hours."

"Sure." Hutchins grunted unhappily.

"Who are you?" Decatur repeated. "You're not with the night riders or I'd be dead by now, I guess. You're not the law—then who? Who the hell else would mix up in this war of ours?"

He didn't get an answer. Morgan looked at Waltham. "Ready to go, Bill? There's a pistol lying over there. Mr. Decatur here owes you an apology, Bill. Maybe if we wait a minute . . . nope, no apology. All right. Let's ease on out. Bill," Shelter nodded toward the staircase behind them. "Lead on, will you? Keep your eyes open."

"I'll keep them open. They're not going to have me again."

"Too bad, Decatur—you lost a good soldier there. Bill was with you all the way. I don't think he'll be back now, do you?"

Decatur wasn't inclined to answer. Morgan nodded and started toward the staircase. Bill was already at the door at the head of the stairs, eyes alert, body crouched and poised.

"Let's go," Shelter said and Waltham opened the door. Nobody—the house was empty as they walked quickly through the living room to the back porch where Shelter had left the marshal's bay horse and Jean's old gelding. He glanced once at the sky, and satisfied that they still had an hour or two of dark, led out.

They rode silently from the town, expecting gunshots behind them at each moment. An hour down the trail they slowed their pace and began finally to relax.

"Tough night," Waltham said.

"You noticed that, did you?" Shelter asked with a grin.

"He was going to kill me. The bastard was going to kill me, you know that?"

"Yes," Shell answered thoughtfully, "I guess he would have done that thing."

"I owe you."

"Not much. My fault you got into this anyway."

"I owe you," Bill Waltham repeated and then for a long while they rode silently through the dark, cold ranks of pines. The ground was frosted, the horses' flanks were rimed, their breath rose in great steamy clouds. The sky was a great fistful of diamonds spattered across the inky vastness.

"Not that way, Bill," Shelter said as Waltham started up the home ranch road. "I took Jean over to Sailor Logan's house. I didn't want to leave her alone. Logan has a daughter so I thought of him."

"You stay one step ahead, don't you?"

"I try. Doesn't always work. You shouldn't have any trouble at home now, I don't think. Decatur seems to be pretty well convinced that I didn't kill his boy. At least he's uncertain. He likely won't come after you again. If you think he will, clear out of the country for a while. Maybe Sailor can bunch your cows with his."

"I'll stay. He won't run me off again," Bill said. "Let's get started though, Jean will be sitting up and worrying if I know her."

"Go ahead on down the trail, Bill. Here's where you and I separate."

"But why?"

"I can't do anything more for you. You've got Jean and your ranch to take care of. I've got my own business.

"All right. Where are you going?"

"Away, Bill. That's all. Maybe we'll meet up again some time and I'll tell you all about it, the whole thing. Right now it's got to be private."

"All right. Thanks again, man. I'd be dead back there if it wasn't for you." Waltham stuck out his hand and Shelter shook it. Then he tugged down his hat and sat in the darkness watching Bill Waltham ride off toward Sailor Logan's. There he had a sister waiting, warmth and friendship, family love. Morgan had none of these ahead of him.

Not in the mountains with the night riders.

12.

From the outcropping on the side of the mountain above Crystal River, the tall dark-haired man could see all the way to Big Dome, all the way to Hogan, though it showed only as a matchbox town with dirty, sulfur-rich smoke rising now and then from the smelters.

In the other direction he could see the Little Utes as those jagged mountains were called, their bare pinnacles thrusting skyward on this cloudless day. A little ranch, the Circle L if he recalled properly, showed as two little red roofs and a tiny, dime-sized silver pond where antlike creatures drank.

The tall man's horse grazed on the lush grass in the narrow alcove cut into the side of the chalky gray cliffs behind him. It wasn't the bay. That had been traded off to a travelling man who had seen enough of this country, enough dead bodies littering the ground. No, this one was a tall black, sound and quick-starting.

The tall man himself looked different. The beard was gone.

The beard was gone and each day for four days he had been spending time with his face turned to the sun, tanning the pallor which had been exposed by the shaving razor's keen edge.

Now Morgan, healed and clean shaven, his shoulder sound, his bruises and knots nearly vanished, grew restless. Anything at all could be happening below him. The night riders could have taken over Hogan; Decatur could have outwitted them, outfought them in a last Armageddon. Somehow Shelter thought that everyone had been doing as he had—lying low.

Decatur had his burdens—the loss of a son, the treachery of the Preacher, the humiliation of being taken prisoner in his own house. He also had his mines to run—and that couldn't be neglected indefinitely. He thought Decatur would be sticking closer to home these days.

And the night riders?

They had been cut up pretty bad at the Ute Trail ambush. Dozens of night riders had fallen that night. They were short on soldiers now, had to be.

Morgan was counting on that.

The sun was bright this morning, bright and warm. Shell rose, walked to where his black stood and removed the hobbles.

"We ride this morning. You ready to put some miles under your belly?"

The horse pricked its ears, listening intently as if by doing so it could decipher this strange human language.

Shelter slipped the bit into the black's mouth, placed the bridle over its nose, fastened the throat latch and picked up his saddle blanket. He whistled as he worked. The sun was warm. Meadowlarks sang off in the long grass. He was going hunting again, and he liked the feeling.

No, that wasn't exactly right—he *didn't* like the danger, the hunting, the killing. He *needed* it. Then he was doing something right and necessary, something no one else, no organ of the law, no army could do.

He found them; he administered justice.

"Exactly what they deserve," someone had once told him. "Not quite," Morgan muttered.

It wasn't quite what they deserved, no. What they deserved was to have their feet slowly frozen, to have their bellies knotted with pain, their fingers amputated, one by one, to have a leg sawn off without the benefit of morphine.

And there were times that a man felt like inflicting that sort of punishment on these criminals from the Conasauga, an eye for an eye it said somewhere, didn't it? Only those who have never had someone near them hurt can afford to be so forgiving as some Shelter had met; but he was no animal, and if it ever got to the point where he hurt them to see their pain, grew evil himself, dark and bitter, then he hoped that someone would stop him with a bullet. He was after all, a human being, and it is a noble experiment of nature, humanity. It wouldn't do to lie down with the animals.

"Let's go," Morgan said to the black, to himself, to the wide day. He swung aboard, feeling light-hearted, ready for most anything.

He had a good horse, a good gun, a cause worth the fighting. There isn't much more a soldier can want. Nothing that didn't come packaged in skirts.

He rode down the narrow Indian trail behind his camp, through the columns of gray, moss-streaked boulders where marmots whistled and played. Away off in the distance a castle of white clouds was building against a deep blue sky. The wind was fresh out of the north, diminishing as Shelter rode into the confines of the long canyon which followed the course of the Crystal River into the western mountains.

His trail crossed the river at a sandbar. Once, it seemed, there had been a bridge there, but no more. Maybe it had been built by a prospector with a claim high in the hills. Now there was nothing but rotting wood and a long cable snarled on itself lying across the creek and in the surrounding willows. Shelter splashed across the river and halted his horse on the far side.

"Easy as pie," he said to the black.

The horse shook its head, its dark mane swirling around its finely muscled neck.

Shelter's remark had been prompted by what he saw impressed on the trail. Three sets of horse tracks, all leading away from Hogan, into the deep mountains where the shadows already lay, where no one rode but the outlaws.

He urged the black forward up a steep incline which debouched onto a wide plateau with an arrow-straight trail running across it toward the purple mountains. Shelter rode on.

The clouds were coming in again, graying as they rode the wind southward. It would rain again, possibly snow. If not tonight, then tomorrow, if not tomorrow, then the day after, but soon. The mountains were deep in shadow, the cold wind rising when Morgan spotted the little red cone of their campfire.

It was coming to dusk, the western sky gray and cold, purple near the horizon, the eastern dark and lifeless. The wind shuffled the long grass and lifted the black horse's mane and tail.

"What do you think?" Morgan asked the horse. "Go on in or wait for an invitation?"

The horse had no strong opinion either way. Shell heeled its flanks and started down the slope toward the campfire as the sky went to deep purple and the nightbirds began to fill the evening sky.

He called out before riding in. The fire was in a small hollow, protected on three sides by rising bluffs. Pines thronged the hills around the hollow. The wind had begun to shriek and howl in earnest.

"Hello the camp!"

"Keep on riding, stranger."

"A friendly way to talk! You got fire there, do I smell coffee?"

"If we got coffee, it's ours. You best head out. There's two Winchesters looking at you now."

"Friend, I'd ride on with that kind of prompting, but we're just going to meet again. We're all riding to the same place, I think," Shelter bluffed. It was just a guess, but where in hell else would anyone be riding in these mountains?

"What do you mean?" a wary voice called back.

"I think you know what I mean. I'm a soldier. Hey, let's talk it over around a cup of coffee. The wind's cold and I've been riding a long way."

There was a long silence, minute upon minute. They must have decided that they had the guns to take care of him anyway, since they finally invited him in. Grudgingly, it seemed, from the tone of voice.

"Come ahead, and come ahead with your hands up."

"All right," Shelter called back. "Easy on those triggers, boys." They were a nervous lot, he decided, and it pleased him. Normally a man would be invited right in to a camp. Sure—it gets lonesome on the trail, not seeing a soul for weeks, months sometimes. These men were not acting normally. If they were nervous they had a reason, and Morgan thought he knew what it was.

Morgan kneed the black forward, holding his hands

high. The animal stopped of its own accord within ten feet of the fire. Glancing around Shelter saw no one. Then slowly they came out of the trees, rifles leveled.

"Shuck those guns, friend."

"Sorry," Morgan said blandly.

"I said toss 'em, or you die," the man snarled. A second voice cut in.

"Easy, Art. Stranger—you'd best get rid of those guns. My friend here doesn't like people backing him up."

"I'm not trying to back him up, but I'm not shedding my guns either, friend. Hell, a man's naked without a gun, ain't he? Besides, like I told you, we're all on the same side. We're all going the same place."

"Are we?"

"Sure. Mind if I swing down? I can do it with my hands raised," Shell said with a grin. There was no answer and so he swung his leg up and over the withers of the black and slipped to the ground, his hands still raised.

"Just hold it right there," one of the men said, but Morgan brazened it out. Ignoring him he walked to the fire, hunkered down and poured himself a cup of coffee in a tin cup he found there. He was sipping it, holding the cup with both hands when the three men came forward to crowd around the fire.

"Cocky, ain't he?" the man to Shell's left asked. "Who the hell you think you are, mister?"

"Why, I don't think who I am. I *know* it. I'm Johnny Court. Out of Denver—don't I know your face?"

No, he didn't know the face. It belonged to a lean, nervous kid with bulging eyes and jerky mannerisms. Nor was Shelter Morgan Johnny Court. He'd never, in fact, seen Court, but a lot of people had. Court was a killer, a stone cold killer who had driven some good lawmen into their graves. He was dead now, was Court, but most folks didn't know that. Morgan did—he had a friend or two in certain places, and he kept his ears open for useful information. Just now it seemed useful to know that Court was dead, to assume Court's identity.

The others seemed to think that Johnny Court was a useful man to have around.

"Why, hell yes. I saw you get Thibedeau in Franklin, Arizona. Johnny Court! This is him, Ed. Damn me if it ain't." This one was positively enthusiastic. He'd never seen Morgan or Johnny Court in his life, but he was anxious to know and to have known. Shelter let his eyes measure the man without seeming to. Well-built, blond, very young as all three were. His eyes were glowing. He thought he was in the presence of a notorious killer and he was liking that.

"You're nuts, Alvin," the nervous one said.

"Hell, Ed, this is Johnny Court, and no one you'd want to mess with."

"Why?" Ed was belligerent. He had come a long way to die and was intent on doing it as quickly as possible. "You've never been to Arizona anyway."

"Sure, the summer I went down with the Lazy Y. Army beef, recall?" It had the sniggering undertones of an adolescent joke. Shelter guessed they had grabbed some steers off somewhere.

"Yeah, well, I guess you were there," Ed said.

"I guess I was!" Alvin was excited. "And Johnny here gunned that sheriff down slick as bear grease."

"That's good enough for me," the third kid said. Young he was, but big as a mountain. He had hands that looked big enough to fit over your skull and crush it like an egg. His name, he said, was Horace Blocker.

"And this here's Alvin Shore," Blocker said, nodding toward the kid who supposed he knew Johnny Court.

"Don't recall you properly," Morgan said, "but I'm glad to meet someone from the old days."

"Sure, Johnny," Alvin said, shaking hands eagerly. "This is my pal, Ed Wingate."

The nervous kid didn't stick out his hand. Morgan marked him as the dangerous one.

"I'm sure as hell glad you're with us, Johnny," Avlin Shore said eagerly. "How the hell did you hear about this job?"

"Same way you did, I reckon," Shelter said casually. Nervous Ed was about to step in here and ask a pointed question, but Alvin blew the game for him.

"Blake, you mean? He found us down in Pueblo cooling our heels. We got that Wells Fargo job on our shoulders, you know," Alvin Shore, who was a very likeable young killer said. "And Wells Fargo got the Pinks on us. We were low and running out of money fast when Blake showed up. He knew us, of course."

"Of course."

"And who doesn't know Johnny Court." Alvin persisted. He was an eager fellow. Eager to kill or be killed.

"Why I must've run into Blake not long after you did," Morgan said, finishing his coffee. "We could've all ridden up together. It's a long trail alone."

"How was Blake's cold when you saw him?" Nervous Ed asked, but Morgan had been waiting for something like that. He had had snares set for him by experts.

"Tell you the truth, if he had a cold I didn't notice it. I wouldn't have noticed if he had green hair and two glass eyes—I was that drunk." He laughed and Alvin Shore, anxious to be accepted by a known gun, joined in, as did Blocker. Nervous Ed didn't even crack a smile.

The conversation went around for a while as darkness settled. Now and then Ed would try to set a trap for

Shelter, but nothing came of it. Alvin had convinced himself that he knew the infamous Johnny Court and the other two were half convinced themselves by now.

"What kind of war are we getting into?" Blocker asked Morgan as the fire burned low.

"Didn't Blake fill you in?"

"He said the pay was good, that we'd be among friends, that there was no law to speak of up here. That's all."

"That's all he could tell anyone," Ed said.

"I thought Johnny might know more."

"A rule's a rule. These boys are close-mouthed," Ed trumpeted. He had a problem. He wanted to be a big man too. All of them did.

Shelter took care not to rub Ed the wrong way. "Well, Blake wasn't supposed to tell me any more, but as I said, I was drinking when he found me and pretty soon we were both drinking and he laid most of this out for me."

Then Shell went ahead and gave them the story of what was happening in those mountains, not bothering to hold anything back. "It's war plain and simple, boys, but there's a lot of gold at stake. We'll outgun them in the end, and those that make it out will make it out wealthy."

"Well," Blocker said, scratching his armpit, "that's all right with me. I seen war of one kind or another since I was fifteen. The thing that worries me is why do they need so many soldiers? What happened to the rest of the gang?"

"They lost a hand to some vigilantes," Shelter said. He poured out the dregs of his coffee into the fire. Steam rose briefly, clouding his dark, somber expression.

"Who in hell's leading this parade, anyway?" Alvin Shore asked. "That's the important thing, ain't it?

Who's bossin' this war? Johnny?"

Shelter shook his head. "No name was mentioned to me. It could be Jesse James for all I know."

"Could be some damned amateur," Blocker growled. "Well, I'm in it for the pay and if that stays good, I'll stick. If I found out they want to use me wrong, well, I guess gold ain't everything."

"I don't get you," young Alvin Shore said. "What do you mean use you wrong?"

"I mean if they've got some jackass runnin' this show that don't know fightin' from spit, I'm haulin' freight. Get me? It's no good workin' for a man that's just goin' to get you killed. Am I right, Johnny Court?"

"You're right," Shelter answered. "There's plenty of work around for a man with a gun. I don't need to take any unnecessary chances."

"Why, sure," Blocker said, well-satisfied with himself. "If I don't like the set-up, why I'll pull out. I'm a Southern boy, but I'm not fightin' for these people because I think there's goin' to be some Confederate States of the West or such—anyone thinks that's a fool. No, sir. I fought for the South; now I'm fighting for Leo Blocker."

And that was the last word on the subject that night. Morgan rolled out his bed some distance from the three would-be gunslingers. He slept with his Colt in his hand, watching the skies twist and reform as the clouds scuttled across the stars.

He felt good about things. Nervous Ed didn't accept him, but the others did. He was Johnny Court, gunslinger, a known man but not a familiar one locally. With the other three as camouflage he could ride right into the outlaw camp. And then . . . and then could come later. There was an idea working in his mind already, but it wasn't fully formed and it was best to see how things lay before committing himself to it.

"Want something?" Shelter asked softly. The dark silhouette was near him, cutting its shape against the sky. Shell's hand tightened around the Colt.

"It's just me. Ed." The voice was a little more nervous than ever. He had a right to be nervous. It wasn't good practise to go walking around a dark camp where armed men were lying.

"What is it, Ed? Trouble?"

"No, Johnny. No trouble. Just seeing to my horse."

"Good. Go back to bed now, Ed, will you?"

"Sure," Nervous Ed said. "Sure." And Morgan saw him retreating silently toward his roll. Shelter grinned. Ed maybe wasn't to be trusted, but he wasn't to be greatly feared. He was the kind that needed a leader, a crowd around him, a specified target. He wasn't the kind to come up to Morgan face to face.

Which didn't mean he wasn't capable of doing it from behind. Not if he had a reason.

Ed wasn't convinced he was Johnny Court. Would they be at the night rider camp? Maybe he had chosen the wrong name. There could well be people there who knew Court on sight . . . there could even be a man there who knew Shelter Morgan on sight.

And that, he thought as he rolled over, drawing his blanket up to his ear, would be the end of that.

13.

They were into the high mountains now. Beyond the Big Dome they began to thrust skyward in ever-ascending rows. Pine edged, silver and green in the morning light, the mountains crowded around them.

The grass was long and thick, water was plentiful. The sky had held back the rain it promised as the four volunteer night riders rode through their second day together.

"Well?" They had halted to water their horses at a narrow rill. Blocker sat his horse, the others had stepped down. It was Blocker who had spoken. "Where the hell is their damned camp? The trail's long gone and we're lost unless Johnny Court here has an idea."

"I've got no more idea than you have," Morgan answered.

"Hell of a way to run an operation," Blocker snorted.

"Easy, Leo. They can't hardly put up a sign." Alvin liked that one. He laughed it up. Shelter wiped out his hatband and replanted his hat, tucking his red kerchief away.

"Men," he said, "I think our problems are over."

They looked around toward the south. To the south where the six men rode out of the timber, slowly moving toward them, all wearing dark rain slickers, all of them with their hats tied down against the wind.

"If this ain't them it should be," Nervous Ed said.

"If it ain't them, it's vigilantes," Alvin Shore added. He unbuttoned his coat and let his hand settle near his gun.

"Don't do anything crazy," Shelter cautioned him.

"I'm not, but if there's trouble, I'll fight."

"Sure. Let's just avoid trouble."

Morgan's eyes were constantly moving, searching the woods beyond the approaching riders, shuttling to Nervous Ed and Blocker, back to the night riders, if that was what they were.

"Could just be cowboys," Nervous Ed said.

"Could be meadow fairies."

They were neither. The riders halted with the sounds of creaking leather, horses shifting their feet and blowing loudly through their nostrils. The man in the lead had a hatchet face and a Missouri drawl.

"You boys lost or somethin'?"

"Not much," Shelter answered. The Missourian had fixed his eyes on Shell, apparently deciding he was the dangerous one there. "A friend of ours said we might ride up this way and get us a little work."

"Do tell?" The Missourian shrugged and wiped at his nose with the back of his hand. "He have a name? This friend."

"Blake," Morgan said. "Blake was his name."

"Blake, huh?" He looked the four newcomers over.

"All right. Why don't you boys fall in with us then. We're riding up home right now."

Shelter agreed and, exchanging glances with the others, he tightened his cinches and swung up. There wasn't the ghost of a smile on any of the faces of the slicker-clad strangers. Night riding, apparently, didn't lend itself to a good sense of humor.

They rode north by west, toward a hulking gray knob of a hill which protruded like a spur from the base of a mountain nearby. There pines crowded the ridges, but the flanks were slick, gray, barren.

"What's that called?" Shelter asked the Missourian. He nodded at the rocky tower.

"Why?"

"A man likes to know where he is."

"Sutler's Tooth they call it. What do they call you?" The Missourian turned his head and spat, then he looked back to Shelter. It was all done off-handedly, but if the night rider didn't like the answer it could mean a sudden end to this trail.

It was too late to change horses now. "Johnny Court," Morgan answered casually. "How 'bout you?"

"Georgia?" he asked and Shelter felt a strange quiver crawl up his spine.

"What?"

"Are you up out of Georgia?"

"No. Tennessee." There wasn't much point in lying about that. "Near to the line though."

"You fought then. You were on the right side."

"I guess I was."

"You were Gray!" The Missourian showed some passion. His dark, hawkish face got very tight. Down in Missouri they hadn't quite given up the war yet. "That was the right damned side, wasn't it?"

"Sure it was."

"You damned right it was! Slavery—they talk about slavery? Why, what in hell do you call the position the government's put the white man in now? Slaves to them and their policies. Give our women away, put the damned dark ones in the state capitol. Rub our noses in it, boy! But you know what? I got a gun, my friend. I got a gun and when they take it out of my dead hand *then* the war is lost."

Morgan accepted all of that silently. Most of the night riders were going to be drifters, men working for a wage, scoundrels. But the Missourian was a different story. He believed in the Cause. That made him a little more dangerous than the rest.

They rode now into the long canyon beside the Sutler's Tooth where the wind, twisted and tormented by the curving jutting landforms, howled and shrieked endlessly. They rode in shadows, single file, slowly.

The Missourian hadn't as much as lifted an eyebrow when Shelter claimed to be John Court, the gunman. Maybe he had never heard of Court. Maybe he was simply biding his time.

The canyon opened now onto a long valley where sparse grass dusted the whitish earth to pale yellow-green. On the rocks above the trail sunlight struck something metallic and dangerous. Shelter glanced up casually. Yes, there would be a guard or two up there, more across the trail. Looking ahead now he could see no other way out of the canyon which was shaped like a spoon with the trail being the handle. All around gray, pine-stippled bluffs crowded against the valley.

Morgan saw more horses now, grazing on the valley floor or corraled behind poles. There were three buildings ahead, all partly of stone, partly of log construction as if someone had come in and added on to older, smaller buildings which was very likely what had happened.

"That's the bunkhouse," the Missourian said, nodding toward a sixty- or seventy-foot long building to their left. "Home for a time."

"Is the boss here?" Shelter asked. The Missourian didn't like the question. His head jerked around sharply.

"I'm boss enough for you for now."

"Sure." Shell shrugged amiably.

"Settle your gear and horses. Catch up on your rest. When you need to know something, someone will let you know. The boys in the bunkhouse will fill you in on anything important."

"Aren't we going to talk to someone?" Alvin Shore put in rather irritably.

"I'm someone, kid. You're talking to me," the Missourian said. "Now—what've you got to say?"

"Nothin'," Alvin said and then he dropped his eyes in subservience and the Missourian knew he had him whipped as a wolf knows a belly-up wolf is nothing to fear.

"Fodder for our ponies?" Blocker asked.

"Ask around."

The Missourian didn't have time to be bothered with trivialities, apparently. He slapped spurs to his roan and it bounded into motion, trailing dust into the face of the following men.

Shelter sat there with his travelling companions, letting the dust settle over them.

"Friendly bastard," big Leo Blocker said.

"Don't matter," Nervous Ed said. "Like you were saying, if it doesn't work out, we ride, huh? We just cut the cord and vamoose."

"That's right," Alvin Shore agreed. But he looked to Shelter Morgan for encouragement and got none. The eyes of the tall man suggested something Alvin already feared—you didn't ride out of this camp unless

146

they let you.

They unsaddled their horses and put them up in the corral behind the bunkhouse. Shelter noticed the piles of tincans and empty boxes back there, the garbage thrown to one side. These men wouldn't have lasted long in any outfit he ran, he decided.

The horses were a different matter. They were simply the best to be had in this part of the country. Bought or stolen, they were well-fed, well-groomed, well-bred and ready to run.

"This ain't exactly the welcome I was expectin'," big Leo Blocker said as the men tramped toward the door of the bunkhouse, saddles over their shoulders. "You'd think they was doin' us a favor."

"If it gets bad, Leo," Morgan said, "We'll pull our freight and that's that."

"Yeah—they won't like that a bit."

"They don't have to. We'll stand together, the four of us, all right? If they don't like it, why they can go to fighting."

"Sure," Leo said. He had accepted Morgan as a leader immediately as had Alvin Shore. "That's the way it'll be. The four of us, and if they don't like it we'll haul our asses out of here. There's plenty of work the four of us could do on our own, I reckon."

"That's right," Morgan said, "but let's give it a chance first, huh? Give it a chance, men, there might be some gold in it."

If there was it didn't show on the men inside the low, dark barracks. There were windows notched out high on the walls at long intervals, one log in thickness. Through these the light from the gray day outside filtered to illuminate the dark, dour features of the men who lay sprawled on the bunks.

It gave Shelter an uneasy feeling of a place seen or visited before, and then he realized what it reminded him of. That Maryland prison, that damned cold, gray bastion inhabited by cold, gray ghostly men. There where he had wasted away seven long years after someone somewhere had pulled strings and gotten him convicted on a spy charge. There where men froze and starved and died as they had on the battlefield. Where the humane saviors of the Nation had allowed a portion of the *31,000* Confederate soldiers who perished in Union prisons to shrivel and shrink and die. They talked about Andersonville now and how the Yankee soldiers had died, but you didn't hear a word about the Union prisons. You've got to dig a little to find out what happened. The Yankees controlled the official version of the war and its causes. Only in the minds of those who had suffered and fought, lived through it, was the truth harbored. And when these were all gone? Well, there's only be the damned Washington versions of what had happened and why and how the evil of the South had been stamped out.

"Any bunk?" Shelter asked a dry, shrivelled man with a crooked scar.

"Any but mine, friend."

"How about this one?"

"Any, friend," the man said again.

Morgan shrugged and tossed his bedroll onto the leather strapped bed. The thin mattress was rolled up at one end, tied with twine. He cut the twine and the mattress snaked open. It was no thicker than Shell's hand, but he had seen worse, he had seen a lot worse.

"Why don't you take another bed, Ace?" The voice was a deep one and Morgan knew before he turned that he would be looking at a big man. He was. Cold-eyed, blocky, thick through shoulders and chest, he had the dull, challenging expression of the natural bully.

"Sure," Morgan shrugged, picking up his bedroll again. Alvin Shore looked at Morgan as if he had been betrayed. Surely Johnny Court wouldn't move for any man.

Johnny Court wouldn't. Johnny Court was also dead.

Morgan moved down the line and found another bunk. A poker game in progress at a half-moon table against the far wall had stopped as interested eyes shifted to Morgan and his new acquaintance.

"Not there," the big man said to Morgan after he had placed his bedroll on another bunk. "That's not for you, Ace." He looked to his friends and winked. Well, there probably wasn't much in the way of entertainment around here. They had to make the best of what they had. A few snickers escaped the card players as Morgan lifted his bedroll again.

"Got any suggestions where I might sack out?" Morgan asked. He was getting tired of the game. He had given the big man what he wanted, a small victory. He had given it to him because it just wasn't worth fighting and dying over. If it made him feel like the bull of the woods, fine. Shell just wanted to throw his roll somewhere and get on with the business at hand.

"Up there, Ace," the big man said. He crowded close to Morgan and lifted his eyes to the upper bunk. He smelled, Shelter found, of onions and leather and sweat—and he smelled strongly of all three. It wasn't real romantic.

"That's Johnny Court you're foolin' with," Alvin Shore called out. It was the worst thing he could've done. A gunman with Court's reputation wouldn't be expected to take this kind of treatment. For Morgan to play Court he was going to have to cut the big man down.

"Johnny Court? Do tell, and I thought you were a tough one," the big man said.

"That bunk?" Shelter said, stilling his impulse to

take the war to this stupid hulk's area.

"Sure, Ace." The dull little eyes glittered. Morgan swung his bedroll onto the top bunk.

"All right?" Morgan asked.

"Well . . ." the big man rubbed his chin and winked at the card players. "Now that I think about it . . ." He reached up and yanked Morgan's bedroll to the floor. It fell between them, and the smell of bay rum seeped out. Morgan's last bottle had just been shattered.

Shell took a slow, deep breath. Johnny Court wouldn't have taken that, no man who called himself a man would. He just shook his head and slowly unbuckled his gunbelt, tossing it to Alvin Shore.

"I believe I'll take this bunk," Morgan said. "Why don't you put my bedroll back up for me. It seems you've accidentally knocked it down."

"I don't do nothin' accidental. My name's Bull Hennessey. When I knock you down it won't be accidental. When I stomp you, boy, it'll be on purpose."

Hennessey supposed Morgan would know his name, and Shelter did. It was said that Hennessey had taken on three miners in a Dakota bar and killed them all bare handed, stomping one to death in front of half the town.

"I didn't get your name," Morgan said. "But that's all right. We don't need names, do we? I'm the man who's telling you to pick that bedroll up, and you're the one who's going to do it, isn't that right?"

"Sure, pal," Hennessey said. His dark eyes shone with excitement now. He was going to get to do somebody, to gouge out eyes, to twist an arm until it broke and splintered, to kick the man until his kidneys ruptured. It was the sort of moment Bull lived for.

He didn't bother to roll up his sleeves. Bull stepped in and arced a terrifying overhand right at Shelter's head, but Morgan went under and to one side, blocking it with his left hand while his right came up and caught Bull Hennessey in the gut.

The big man didn't even seem to feel it. It was like punching a grizzly bear.

"We're going to have some fun, my friend," Bull said, and he came in again.

Bull tried to hang another right on Shell's jaw, but Morgan blocked it neatly, backed away and came in with three straight jabs which rocked Bull's head back.

In surprise and amusement Bull Hennessey grinned, turned his head and spat out a trickle of blood from a cut lip.

"You goin' to be all right, boy. You and me goin' to be all right. I don't like 'em too easy, you know."

Hennessey came in again. A short left grazed Shell's temple and then Bull's boot lashed out, thudding against Morgan's knee. The pain was momentarily crippling and he found himself unable to step aside as Bull came in winging rights and lefts from the floor, uppercuts meant to decapitate a man. The force of those big shoulders was ominous but Morgan managed to block or bob away from three of the blows before a fourth landed with staggering force, twisting Shell's head around, driving him back against the wall, the blood leaking from his mouth and nostrils as Bull Hennessey came in, flat-footed, inplacable, monstrous.

He grabbed Shelter by the shirt and yanked him forward, trying to draw him into an upcoming knee but Shell twisted away, leaving a part of his shirt in Bull's hand. With his back to the bunk Morgan jabbed out again, twice, three times, tried a sneaky right from underneath and was disappointed as it failed to connect.

Bull was still grinning. The man was an ape, a fighting machine. He lived to punish, to kill, and he came in again, letting a big right hand shot fly.

Morgan stepped back, grabbed the rail of the upper bunk and toppled the beds in front of Bull, slowing him down a little. Shell backed up toward the far wall. The poker players still sat watching, enjoying themselves. It didn't take a lot to entertain these fellows.

Bull stepped through and over the bed and lunged toward Morgan. Shell stepped to his left and tripped over a foot thrust out by one of the card players. He went down hard, his bad shoulder and skull both slamming against the plank floor of the bunkhouse.

Bull Hennessey was all over him. He lifted a big booted foot, wanting to stomp Shelter to bloody paste. Morgan rolled his head to one side and managed to catch the boot with his hands as it whistled by. Shell's fingers were ground against the floor, but he gathered himself and shoved. Bull Hennessey toppled over backwards, his back crashing against the poker table, scattering chips, cards and players. For a minute it seemed the big man might not get up, but he did, slowly lifting himself from the floor. There was a grin on his face still, a dull, savage grin. He was enjoying himself at last. Bull Hennessey hadn't even started yet.

14.

Shelter Morgan leaned against the wall, panting heavily. His fingers were torn and bloodied. His head rang from the hammerlike blows of Bull Hennessey. He had thrown his best punches at the big man and hadn't managed to faze him.

"Now, Ace," Bull said as he came forward, his arms hanging, his fists bunched. "Now you buy it."

Bull came in with a chopping left, a short, digging right which landed hard against Shell's side as he backed away still jabbing, kicking out from time to time, trying to break Bull Hennessey's kneecap for him.

Twice Morgan kicked the big man solidly, twice he landed jarring right hand hooks against the jaw of the plodding Bull Hennessey, but it didn't slow him up at all. He came on, machinelike, a great windmill with fists wildly, inexorably swinging past Morgan's face so that it took every bit of skill, all of his concentration to dodge the sledge hammering blows.

Morgan felt the wall against his back and he braced himself, waiting. He almost wished now he had chosen guns when Bull had challenged him. Almost, but not quite. Whatever sort of animal Bull Hennessey was he didn't deserve a bullet through the brisket for a trifling bit of bullying.

"Come on in," Shelter said, beckoning with his fingers. He was grinning now, but a lot of that was bluff. He just didn't have the physical tools to handle a man like Bull Hennessey. He was twice Shelter's size through the shoulders and chest and had the thighs of a circus strongman. Shelter's only chance was to wear him down, and that might take as long as the sea took to wear a rock away.

"Let's see what you got, Bull. What's the matter, running out of steam?"

"Why damn you, you fool. You're going to die, can't you see that? Right here, right now. I'm going to pound you to dog meat."

Enraged, the big man came in again, swinging wildly, rushing his blows. Nevertheless he was throwing punches that were hard enough to powder rock and when Morgan caught one on the chin he went down.

He went down and that scared him. Bull was a stomping man and he had Shell down again. A kick sang past his skull as he rolled to his knees trying to clear his head, to fend off another kick. Somewhere up above the menacing boots, like a face seen through the wrong end of a telescope, was the grinning moron face of Bull Hennessey.

Suddenly Shelter was angry. No, he was mad as hell—this subhuman brute wanted to take his life away from him. His life! For what, an affair of honor? For the love of a woman, a blood grudge, a duty to a warring nation? Hell, no, for his entertainment.

It was cheap and it was filthy and it was maddening. Morgan got to his feet, his back to the wall as his legs, rubbery under him stood fixed and braced. Bull Hennessey came in again.

"You look tired, boy, damned tired," Hennessey said. "I got you, boy. I got you now."

Shell saved his breath. As Bull tried to tag him he dropped one shoulder and countered with a right which hit Bull on the temple solidly. It was a hard enough blow to cause bone to crack in Shell's hand and Hennessey showed the effect of it. He staggered just momentarily, but stagger he did and there was fresh purpose, fresh anger on his face when he came in.

He didn't like Shell being against the wall—he had to pull his punches or break his own hands. He tried grabbing Morgan by the shirt, pulling him away but a stiff left to the face caught him on the nose and he backed away, blood leaking darkly from his nostrils.

"Damn you!" Bull didn't like the taste of his own blood and his eyes lit up. He came in hard, wading into Shell with lefts and rights digging into the ribs. Morgan blocked three of them but a fourth hit home with shocking force, driving the wind from his body, stunning the heart.

Morgan had to move. Hennessey was draped all over him and so he ducked and turned away, leaving the wall to Bull Hennessey as Morgan showed him how to jab and move. Jabbing and moving was all Morgan could do right then and so he stuck with it. Two lefts and a sidestep, ducking and bobbing away as Bull's massive fists cut air beside Shell's ears.

He was tiring. The big man was tiring and both of them knew it. His punches, never crisp, now came muddling through the space between them.

"You're out of shape, Bull," Morgan taunted.

"You ought to give it up, man. You're too old for anything but a one-shot fight and some stomping."

Bull roared with savage anger and lunged toward Shell. Morgan caught him with a right hook flush on the ear and he laughed out loud with barbaric pleasure as Bull stumbled and had to drop his hands as he started toward the floor.

Morgan had Bull off balance and he had started down but Shell backed away from him. It wasn't going to be that easy for Bull. He had done all the giving, now he was going to do some of the taking.

There was enough strength in the man to land a solid left on Shell's neck, enough to drive through Morgan's defenses with a thudding right, but the sting was gone, that pile driving explosiveness and Morgan only grunted, taking the punches as he gave his own, exchanging Bull's heavy, softening blows for his razor-like stabbing jabs and quick crossing rights.

Shell landed two in a row on the point of Bull's chin, sharp, jabbing punches which snapped the big man's head back. Bull stepped away, not liking it at all. Morgan whistled in a right hand lead and split the flesh on Bull's cheek open to the bone. The cut was only an inch long but it bled furiously and again the feel of his own blood flowing spurred Bull to action, but he just didn't have it, he had lost it somewhere along the line.

He came in swinging roundhouse punches which Shell picked off as he backed away, stabbing that cutlass-like left into Bull's face. Bull's blood had spattered both of them. Bull's face was swollen and cut, puffy around the eyes. Morgan didn't imagine he looked much better.

Only now could Shell hear the clamor of voices around them, now as his attention slackened and his second wind came back, as his senses were able to afford less concentration, as he backed Bull toward the far wall, cutting him to pieces with lacing shots from either hand.

"Come on, Bull! Fight back, big man!"

"Christ, I hope he kills him."

"Go on, Johnny. Lay him out!"

Morgan grinned as he belatedly realized that he was Johnny. Johnny Court, the gunman. He did what they wanted Court to do. It came easily, quickly. A left hook which caught Bull Hennessey on the hinge of the jaw. Bull just plain stopped in his tracks. His eyes rolled back then down. He lifted a hand, gurgled something at Morgan and then went down, his hand clutching the blankets on the bunk beside him, pulling them down in a tumble on top of him as he collapsed on the floor and stayed there. Morgan stepped forward and tugged the blanket up over his head. Slowly then he looked around. You never knew when a man had friends with guns ready to finish the fight the way they wanted it.

Either Bull had no friends that close or the knowledge that Morgan had three travelling companions of his own had stifled any such thought.

"Anyone else?" Morgan asked.

There wasn't any answer. They had seen enough of Morgan.

"Alvin, will you throw my gear on my bunk? I've got to wash up."

"Sure, Johnny. Hey, Johnny? How come you didn't just shoot him?"

"And waste a bullet?" Morgan grinned and the kid grinned in return. He was a good kid, Shell thought, wondering vaguely what had ever started Alvin Shore and his friends down the wild and very short outlaw trail. A night of whisky and some game with firearms? Likely.

Shell found his hat and put it on. He walked out the door and into the cold glare of late sunlight. The watering trough had a pump beside it, and hanging his hat on the limb of the broken cottonwood tree which shaded the trough, he pumped the rusty handle.

It squeaked shrilly and on the third try gave loose a gout of icy water which Shell ducked his head under, washing the back of his neck, his aching head, rinsing the blood from his eyes.

Finished, he straightened up, shook his head, smoothed back his hair and stood staring up at the high mountains which surrounded the little valley. His hands were very sore, and he was pretty sure he had gotten a knuckle broken. Fortunately it was on the left hand. Unfortunately it ached like hell as did ribs and belly, head and neck, shoulders and legs.

The wind was cold on Shelter who stood there in drenched clothing, his shirt torn, and he started back toward the bunkhouse, snatching up his hat from the cottonwood limb.

"Court!" The voice called out and Shelter tensed, readying himself for a bigger game than he had played with Bull Hennessey. "Hey, Johnny Court."

Morgan glanced toward the voice and then turned. It was the Missourian, waving his hand, striding toward the trough. Shelter stood and waited. The wind played with the leaves of the cottonwood, sere and brown. The sky darkened as dusk came on and the clouds drifted in again.

"What is it?"

"I didn't know who you were, Court," the Missourian said, "sorry about that."

"Sure. Nothing to it."

"You all settled in to the bunkhouse?"

"Just about. Made a few new friends."

"I'll say you did—you look like it. Who was it?"

"Bull Hennessey he called himself."

"Bull . . . Christ! And you're walking around?

Where's Bull?"

"Resting." Shelter inclined his head toward the bunkhouse. "Last time I saw him he was resting."

"Like I say, I didn't know who you were, Court. I guess you've got some kind of reputation, huh?"

"You know how that is."

"Yeah, I guess I do, but up at the house they think you deserve yours. That is, they want you up there."

"Meeting?" Shelter looked toward the big house which sat on the low knoll above and fifty yards beyond the bunkhouse and corrals.

"Yeah. Grab your gear. You won't be stayin' down here with the cheap help."

"All right. The boss is here now, is he?" Shelter asked. He asked it casually but his gut was knotting up. The boss—the man with a silver-inlaid Colt, the man Shell had been chasing for two thousand miles and ten years. Kyle Cornelius.

"No," the Missourian said, "but he's coming in tonight. Something big is up and they want you in on it."

They had reached the bunkhouse now and the Missourian stepped in first. There was Bull Hennessey before him, sitting on a lower bunk, his bloody face in his hands.

"Resting, huh?" the Missourian asked. Bull didn't even lift his head.

"What's up?" Alvin Shore sidled up to Morgan as he collected his saddle and gear from the newly-made bunk. "There's not going to be any trouble over the fight?"

"No. Nothing at all, Alvin. They want me to sleep up at the big house, that's all."

The kid was relieved. "Good. Johnny, we were ready to stand with you, you know. Me and Ed and Big Leo."

"Sure. How 'bout next time, Alvin?" Shelter settled

those blue eyes on Alvin. The kid shook his head in bewilderment.

"I don't get you, Johnny," Alvin said. "You told me there was no trouble brewing."

"No. Not now. You've seen men like me, Alvin. Wherever I go there seems to be trouble. The best thing you three can do is saddle up and get the hell out of here. Second best is to stay away from me. The worst thing you can do is to talk yourself into siding me, Alvin. There's going to be trouble, yeah, and you boys aren't ready to handle it." Shelter rested a hand on the kid's shoulder for a moment. "Stay loose, kid. Get the hell out of this game if you can."

He shouldered his saddle before Alvin could answer, turned on his heel and walked out, the Missourian in his tracks. Alvin Shore stood and watched the tall man go out, watched the door close behind him.

"What was that about?" Leo Blocker asked.

"Damned if I know. He's a funny man, is Johnny Court. Know what he told me? To get the hell out of here and out of the game."

Blocker was thoughtful. He spent a second or two biting at his lip before he said, his voice low and sincere. "Alvin, Johnny Court is a man who knows a thing or two. I've spent some time lately myself thinking that maybe we're not cut out for this."

"When?" Alvin asked.

"Tonight. After dark, let's blow this place if we can. The folks still got a place down in Texas. We'll gather up Ed and head out. Unless . . ."

Alvin was still looking at the door. "No," he shook his head, "I'm willing. Court is right. There's something here that feels wrong, something that smells like blood and death. I'm for Texas, Leo. Tell Ed not to get himself too settled. There's going to come a killing time here and I don't want to be here when it starts."

160

Shelter Morgan planned on being there when it started.

He looked at the big house which was once white, now nearly colorless, the wood siding gone as gray as the stone which comprised the older section of the house. There was half of a second story as if the builder had run out of funds or patience or need.

Wisteria, now brown and withered, climbed unpainted trellises on either side of the porched front door. There was a dead pine tree to one side, an unused stone well on the other. Some sort of ornamental statue stood in the shrubbery near the house, overgrown and hidden by time.

There were no horses visible. The hitchrail was empty.

"No one home?" Morgan asked.

"Oh, yeah. They're home. Like I say, the boss won't be in until midnight or so, maybe later. Say—smell that?" The Missourian lifted his head and smiled appreciatively—though he wasn't very good at smiling, it was more a twisting of the upper lip. "Roast pork, I'll tell you. Boss's got a Chinee cook. Yes, he does!" the Missourian said, enjoying Shell's surprise. "He likes to live well. Brought that Chinee all the way from Denver because he liked his pot pie."

Shelter dropped his saddle and bedroll on the sagging porch, scraped his boots on the iron scraper beside the door and followed the Missourian in.

"Hello! Hell," his guide grumbled. "Where've they got to?"

The house was damp, cool, furnished in a surprisingly luxurious way from the red and gold carpet to the expensive mirrors on the walls, the red velvet draperies. The outside of the house didn't prepare anyone for this.

The two men, carrying their hats, walked into a parlor of sorts where a red velvet settee faced a love seat of the same style. A white wooden mantle roofed over a low-burning, brass-screened fireplace across the room.

"You'd best wait here, Johnny. I'll poke around a little more. Damn them. They want you and then they disappear." The Missourian went off grumbling and Shelter stood by the fire, not entirely comfortable with things. *Who* wanted to see him if the boss was not here? And what exactly did they want to see him about? For all he knew he was going to come face to face with someone who knew Johnny Court, and that was unsettling.

He shifted his Colt in his holster and waited, prepared for almost anything.

For almost anything except what happened.

A door closed somewhere—upstairs, he thought—and a moment's muted conversation drifted through the house to Shelter. He couldn't make anything of it. A moment later he heard the approaching footsteps, rapid and light. The door to the parlor swung open and Shelter's eyes lifted, his body tensed, his hand dropped nearer to his gun butt.

And Miss Gloria Decatur walked regally into the room.

15.

Shelter's mind refused to function for a moment—the last person in the world he would have expected to meet had just flounced into the room, looking cool and competent, wearing a low cut white satin gown that showed off magnificent white breasts, trailed to her ankles and in between managed to form itself enticingly to her curved, efficient looking hips. She fixed cool eyes on Morgan, measuring eyes, haughty and sensual at once, the glittering jewel-like eyes of an adder, the hungry eyes of a wolf.

"Mister Court?" she said and her voice was low and breathy.

"That's right."

Gloria Decatur came nearer, her body swaying, straining against the white satin of her dress. The firelight picked up the facets of the diamonds she wore at her throat, at her wrists, and filled Morgan's vision with dancing highlights. The woman's auburn hair shone like burnished copper.

"You can call me Gloria."

She had halted an inch or two away from Shell, her breasts within a hair's breadth each time she inhaled, which was more often than normal respiration would dictate. Her breathing was rapid and shallow, her eyes shining and beckoning.

"All right, Gloria." Morgan looked around the room, growing uncomfortable, fearing a trap.

"No, there's no one here but the Chinese cook and the maid. Do I make you nervous, Johnny Court?"

"Yes, Gloria, you do." What was she thinking? Did she know him or not? They had only met once, and that had been at a distance. Morgan had had his beard on then, however, and this would be the last place she would expect to see Marshal J.T. Forsberg appear.

"Don't let me frighten you. I like you. I saw you ride up and I liked you. Then I found out who you were and it excited me. Do you know what I mean? That's the kind of woman I am, Johnny. Danger excites me. Danger and pain and killing. I like my men dangerous."

"I understand, I suppose," Morgan said, "but . . ."

"But what? You've got a gun," she said casually. "Suppose someone told you to leave me alone? Why, you could kill them, couldn't you?"

Yes, he thought. I could kill them and you'd wet your panties with excitement. There was something very wrong with Gloria Decatur. Is that what she was doing here with the night riders, the gang that was robbing her father blind, seeking excitement, the crazy thrills of death and brutality?

"You don't like me at all," the woman said petulantly, spinning away to walk to the red settee where she sat, one foot propped up on the cushions, the other stretched out on the floor, glaring at Morgan.

"Do you like me? Do you?"

"Yes, ma'am, Gloria—I just didn't expect this, you see."

"I know. That's why I did it. I like something sudden, something to stir me up. I've always been like that. Look here, Johnny, how long have you been on the trail? How many nights did you spend dreaming of something like this?"

Morgan could only stand and stare. The woman had slowly hiked her dress up over her knees and now as Shell's eyes travelled the length of her beautiful, magnificently tapered, strong legs, she spread her legs wider and opened herself to his view. A long white, ringed finger dipped into her nest of auburn colored hair and stroked the glistening pink lips of flesh there as Morgan feeling aroused, trapped, threatened and sickened all at once looked toward the door of the room.

"I told you there's no one here," Gloria said and her voice was deep and heavy, almost effortful. "Are you going to make me play with myself all evening?"

"No. But not here," Morgan said, taking what seemed to be the only reasonable way out. "You've got a room."

"I thought here," Gloria said, bending forward to look at herself as she spread and stroked her tender flesh. "By the fire." She was petulant and . . . drugged? The idea passed through Shell's mind. He had seen women on opium before and their behavior was not a lot different. But no, Gloria wasn't drugged or drunk. She was only, he thought, a little mad.

He crossed the room to her, stretching out his hand. No matter what he wanted to get out of here—her idea of sexual excitement wasn't the same as his, apparently. He didn't want to have to kill somebody so that she could get her thrills.

"Come on. Upstairs. Is that where your room is?"

"Not here?" Gloria asked sulkily.

"No. Come on. Show me your bedroom."

"A traditionalist. I'm surrounded by them. Always on the bed."

"On the floor, on the dressing table, on the roof if you want, but not here."

Shell helped her to her feet and she fell against him, her tongue darting between his lips filling his mouth as she ground herself against him. She fell away then, looking up at him, and her hand dropped briefly to his crotch, cupping the rising erection there. She smiled smugly and tugged at his hand, leading him toward the door.

The hallway beyond was empty. The stairs on the left led up to a dark second story. Outside the sun was behind the mountains, the gray clouds had gone black and a light, lashing rain had begun.

Shelter Morgan was inside and he was playing with fire. There was something demonic about this woman, deeply dangerous, unpredictable. It scared him, honestly scared him.

She opened the door to her bedroom and went in, leaving the door standing open. Morgan closed it and locked it behind them. Gloria turned, smiled and unpinned her hair which fell in an auburn cascade across her shoulders.

"Light that lamp, will you, Johnny. I want to see that body of yours. I want to eat you with my eyes."

Morgan turned and struck a match, lighting the lamp. When he turned back Gloria had pulled her dress off up over her head. She had nothing on underneath.

"Well?" she said, turning slowly in a circle, her

arms over her head. Her body was magnificently proportioned, nearly round, alabaster breasts with tiny pink buds for nipples, sleek hips and thighs, a downy nest of hair between her legs. Beautiful, perfect, deadly.

"Lovely," Morgan said honestly. "You're a lovely creature."

"Take your pants off, Morgan. Let's see how lovely you are," Gloria said and Shelter did so. What, he wondered, would Johnny Court do? Something very similar, he thought.

He peeled off his torn shirt, kicked off his boots and dropped his trousers. A small sigh of pleasure escaped the lips of Gloria Decatur.

"I want that," she said. "I want that crammed in me. Oh, yes. Please, let me have it."

Shelter started toward her. She had eased back toward a low dressing table where perfumes and powders sat. She swept them all aside with one gesture of her hand and sat down on the table, spreading her legs, lifting them until her heels were resting on the table as well, her knees out wide like wings and she dipped anxious fingers into her own warmth, eagerly stroking her hungry body as she watched Shell's approach, her eyes fixed on his swollen shaft, the bull-like sack pendulous between his legs.

"Get over here, damn you," she croaked. "Look at this empty thing, Johnny Court. Look there, it needs you inside, filling me."

Shelter didn't argue with the lady. He took another three steps and Gloria's trembling hand reached out and gripped his erection, leading him toward her, her breath very rapid, frenzied as she craned her neck toward him, wanting his kiss, his touch.

Morgan met her lips, felt the soft darting of her tongue, an adder's kiss, felt her take the head of his shaft and insert a bare half an inch of it into her warmth, a bare half an inch which her inner muscles worked at, hungrily playing against it as her lips worked at his.

"Johnny, fuck me hard, please. Ram it home, and now—what are you waiting for!"

Shell eased in and she clutched at his buttocks, her fingernails digging into the flesh, her legs going around him as her kiss became more intent.

"Now, I want to feel it now," she whispered and then her teeth clamped down on his ear, bringing blood. She laughed, bucking at him, her legs locked around him as her pelvis ground against his.

She bit him again, very hard. "Won't you hit me, Johnny? Hit me back. Ruin me. Split me wide open. Oh, that's better Johnny! I want it all the way inside, all of you. Everything." She clutched at his sack again, her fingers pressing him against her hot flesh.

"Let me go!" She practically screamed it out and Shelter loosened his grip on her. Gloria slid off him, landing on the floor beside him on her knees. "Pull my hair," she said and Morgan could only stand looking down at her. "Hit me, please."

She had one hand on her own crotch and she worked her body against it. The other hand clung to Shell's thigh as her tongue ran up his leg and down again, as she moaned and writhed and worked out some private fantasy.

She took his hand then and tugged him down, down onto the hard floor where she got up on hands and knees, her hands reaching around to spread herself to Shell's view.

"In there. Come in from behind, please! Oh, God, I need it now, Johnny."

Morgan eased up behind her, his hands resting on her smooth, silky buttocks. Her grasping fingers found him and positioned him, and he watched himself slide in as Gloria on her knees moaned and went slack, her cheek against the floor, her hair spread out on a burnished fan.

"Again," she said, "again. Again . . ." her voice droned on and on. Shelter rocked against her, hearing her voice distantly, feeling the encouraging fingers, the warm demanding flesh of her body.

When he could take it no more he moved in nearer, filling her savagely with his entire length and she gasped, her mouth going slack. Her hand clutched at his shaft, feeling the pulsing there. She withdrew it, cradling it in her hand, feeling the warmth seep from Shelter Morgan against her soft palm, before, satisfied, she placed it back into the warm nook of her body and lay still until the pounding of her heart slowed, until the drowsy forgetfulness overcame her raw hungers.

Twisted, Morgan thought. Something had happened to her somewhere back down the trail to take her normal healthy desires and twist them into cruel needs. But what in hell was she doing *here?* That was more important to him now than the rest of it.

No wonder, he thought, the night riders knew what the vigilantes were going to do next. Decatur's own daughter was in their camp. Shelter was next to her, the sagging weight of her naked body pressed to his, ripe and smooth, utterly repellant. She didn't have the warmth, the attractiveness a woman, almost any healthy woman might have had. Her flesh might have been marble—her heart certainly was. What man could love this thing?

"Don't move. Don't even try it."

The voice came from the doorway. The door had been locked, but this one had had a key. This one was a quiet, shadowy thing who knew how to move quietly from place to place, a substanceless, deadly man.

There was a look of savage anger on his face, a silver-mounted Colt in his hand.

Bill Waltham stepped into the room and leveled the muzzle of his gun at Shelter Morgan.

16.

Waltham stood in the doorway for a long moment, just looking, his face contorted with disgust. He had someone with him, but Morgan couldn't see who it was until Bill gave a yank on a tethering rope and Jean Waltham stumbled forward, her eyes wide, her face bruised, her hands bound. She stared at Shelter without seeming to see him. Waltham shoved his sister down into a wooden chair where she sat submissively.

"Get up," Bill said. The Colt was steady in his hand, but there was a tremor in his voice. "Get up, you filthy bitch!"

"What are you going to do?" Gloria asked. She was on hands and knees, her auburn hair hanging in her face. Her naked body was smooth and ripe in the lanternlight. "Are you going to kill him!" Excitement mingled with horror in her voice. "Are you going to beat me, Bill!"

Waltham turned away from her. "Get your pants on, Morgan."

"How long have you known?" Shell asked.

"Quite a while. You never gave me the chance to do anything about you."

"The night we met the night riders in that ambush— you were there, on our side."

"That's right." Shelter's eyes were on the gun Bill held, and Waltham got the picture. "You saw someone with my gun? Yeah, it was the Missourian, Pitt. It wouldn't have done for me to wear it when I was with the vigilantes, would it? That was the first night I hadn't been able to slip away before the actual battle."

Morgan was buttoning his shirt, his eyes fixed on the Colt in Bill Waltham's hand, on Jean who seemed battered and broken. "You had to hurt her?" Morgan asked.

"Jean?" Bill shrugged as if it were of no importance. "She knows now. She found out when my men came to Sailor Logan's to get me. We had to burn Sailor out. A couple of the boys had at his daughter. Jean didn't like it. Sisterly feeling, I guess."

"Are you going to kill him?" Gloria asked again. "Kill him, or let me do it, slow and easy, kill him again." She got to her feet and started toward Bill.

Kill him again? Morgan couldn't put a handle on that one until he recalled the mutilated body of J.T. Forsberg, the multiple wounds which indicated torture and slow death—yes, she would be the type.

"You guessed?" Waltham asked casually. "Yeah, it was Gloria. We caught that son of a bitch of a marshal. Him with a tin badge and his warrants, coming to arrest me!" Bill Waltham—Kyle Cornelius—laughed harshly.

"So you threw him to Gloria."

"That's right, Captain. It gave her a little pleasure." There was something behind the eyes of Kyle Cornelius, something waiting to come out and scour and smash the world. He was a killing thing poised on the edge of slaughter. Morgan saw that now, saw the killer that was Bill Waltham, was Kyle Cornelius.

"Kill him!" Gloria demanded and she took another step toward Bill Waltham who triggered off.

The Colt boomed in the close confines of the room, shattering eardrums. Gloria was lifted to her toes and then hurled back against the wall. Jean Waltham screamed as Gloria slid slowly to the floor, her blood streaking the wall behind her, her eyes wide with terror and the knowledge of death. When she hit the floor she lay there burbling bloody bubbles from her nostrils for a minute longer before she died.

"You never could keep your hands off other men, could you?" Bill Waltham said to the dead woman. "I tried to warn you, Gloria. I told you I wouldn't put up with it."

"Me next?" Morgan asked. His teeth were locked together, his fists clenched at his sides.

"Oh, yes. You next, Captain Morgan. I can hardly let you live. But you interest me. You've come a long, long way to die . . ."

The Missourian had appeared in the doorway, hatless, breathless, toting a shotgun, and Waltham turned toward him. "What is it?"

"Everything all right, boss? I heard . . ." Then he saw the body against the floor and he knew.

"Everything's all right. Go on and get the men ready. We're going to ride tonight."

"Sure, boss." The Missourian looked at Morgan, at Jean, and once again at the body before withdrawing.

Waltham crossed the room and perched on the window sill. Behind him rain streaked the window. From time to time distant lightning flashed.

"When did you know who I was?" Morgan asked.

"Almost right away. I knew, after all, that you weren't J.T. Forsberg. It took me a time but I mentally removed the beard and then I had you. You're a tall man, Captain Morgan, taller than most. Your eyes—I recall them well too."

"From the meadow."

"From the meadow, that's right. You should have come in with us, you know. What have you done that's brought the dead back to life? You haven't changed anything at all."

"Maybe not," Morgan said, standing there, staring at Kyle Cornelius. In a way he was the cleverest of them all. And the most vicious. "What about Jean? Where does she fit into this." Morgan looked at the girl, saw her eyes spark, lift to his, saw her head shake. It was no good, she was saying. Life was over.

"She doesn't fit," Waltham—or Cornelius—said. "That's Jean's problem, isn't it? She just doesn't fit."

"She's your real sister?" Morgan asked.

"Yes. My real sister. I know you're playing for time, by the way, Captain Morgan, hoping something will happen to your advantage. But nothing will, I assure you."

"Jean told me her father, your father, was killed by the night riders. She told me she sent for you later."

"Quite true," Cornelius said. "Someone killed my father and I came up here to settle it. I did too. I left my fairly profitable line of endeavor down in Arkansas and proceeded north and west. It took me a while to get the picture, but when I did I moved in some friends and we took charge. The night riders were formed by an idealistic and very senile ex-Confederate named Page Willoughby. He had a nice racket here—the local people protecting him, seeing the old man was a sort of hero of the poor. He had a nice racket but he didn't know how to use it."

"You eliminated Willoughby."

"Yes, of course. And then I moved in here and brought Gloria into our camp. She was looking for someone to lead her to perdition anyway. I happened to be here. Meanwhile I split my time between the night riders and the home ranch, enough to keep Jean satisfied. Nights when she thought I was out watching the heard, we were riding. I even raided my own herd now and then to keep things legitimate appearing."

"But she wrote for help."

"That's right." Bill looked at his sister and shook his head. "She thought I wasn't doing enough and she sent for help. It was a simple matter to eliminate one Marshal Forsberg. But two—you've proven hard to kill."

"Until now," Shell said. He was still looking at Jean Waltham, trying to give her a message, but she was dazed, battered. "Why did you enlist under a phony name, Bill?"

"Why? I already had a record when the war broke out, captain. A killing record. It hadn't gotten to where they were taking jailbirds yet. I had a little book of poetry I used to read as a kid. The man's name was Kyle Cornelius—probably not his real name either—and I took a fancy to it."

Morgan nodded. Nodded wearily. The trail had been long, so long—all the way back to Georgia and the bloody Conasauga. And here he was now facing Kyle Cornelius, and behind him on the floor was the dead woman, the dead *thing*.

"What about Jean, Bill?" That was all he wanted to know now. "What about your sister?"

"She knows it all, doesn't she?" Bill shrugged. "She's got to go. With you and Gloria. Wherever it is you're going. I'd like to stay and talk some more, you know? I honestly would. I heard about some of the men you killed. General Custis—I'd like to hear about that, about the sort of life he was living in that Chinese tong. Alas, there's no time, is there, Morgan?''

"No. I guess not."

Waltham stood away from the window. Outside thunder boomed, shaking the glass in the window frames. Lightning winked on and off. Shelter saw the Colt come up slowly, that silver inlaid Colt, that beautiful, deadly weapon.

From the corner of his eye he saw other movement. Jean twisted in her chair and her booted foot shot out, kicking over the table beside her, the table where the kerosene lantern rested.

"Don't . . . !" Bill Waltham shouted. He switched his sights toward his sister, but Shelter reaching behind him, grabbed the wooden chair and flung it at Waltham.

The chair smashed into his head and upraised arm as the lantern hit the floor and burst into flame. Waltham went down in a heap, cursing, screaming. The silver Colt was no longer in his hand as the tongues of flame following the rivulets of kerosene across the floor leaped to life and illuminated the room brightly, as black smoke curled toward the ceiling.

The draperies caught and Shelter saw Waltham, forearm in front of his face, race toward the door, diving through a sheeting wall of flames. Shell was beside Jean, cutting at her ropes with his bowie. She was dazed still, slow, and Morgan yanked her to her feet, shouldering her as he turned and crossed the room through the choking smoke, the rippling orange flame toward the window.

With one hand Shell snatched up the second chair and hurled it through the window into the rainy night. Ducking low he stepped out onto the sloping roof of the first story, glancing back only once to see the flames engulfing the room, to see the naked, huddled figure on the floor, the lovely, lovely marble of her body glossed by the flames, the hair beginning to singe already. In minutes there would be nothing left of her—nothing anyone would care to see.

Shell walked to the edge of the roof and looked down. The rain drove against him. The night and the yard were dark.

"Jean? I can't jump with you. Can you make it?" He shook her shoulders and felt the strength come back into her, felt her steel herself for whatever lay ahead. She was not a quitter, this one.

"Go ahead. I'll follow," she panted.

Morgan turned and dropped to the ground below to stand looking up, half-expecting a shot in the back. Bill had had time to get downstairs, to alert his army . . . Jean dropped into his arms. Shelter took her hand and together they raced across the muddy yard as the back door of the house burst open and Waltham and the Missourian stood momentarily framed in the doorway, lighted by the lamp within. What Morgan would have given for a rifle at that moment—but he had none and they could only run, keep on running as the upper story of the house exploded with scarlet and orange flame which frothed against the rainy skies.

They raced toward the circle of oaks which stood beyond the narrow barn behind the house, and reaching it they stood panting together, cold and defenseless.

"What now?" Jean asked. Lightning forked downward striking near at hand. The pale light illuminated her face with ghastly intensity.

"A horse and a gun."

"We'll never get out of here. He's got fifty men."

"We'll never survive if we don't try. If they find us here you know what's going to happen."

"He's my brother," Jean said irrelevantly. He was her brother, yes, but he was a sick man, a deadly killer.

Bill and Gloria Decatur—what a team that had been, what a partnership, ending in the only way it could end, with one venomous head striking the other.

Shelter dropped to the ground, taking Jean with him. The Missourian had somehow gotten close to them, very close. Now he showed plainly against the blazing inferno behind him—the whole house was going up, rain or none. The upper story was near to collapse.

The night was a wild mixture of fire and smoke, rain and wind. Through this the Missourian moved, looking right and left, seeing shadowy targets everywhere, not seeing the man who lay nearly at his feet. Shelter Morgan who now lunged forward, launching himself at the Missourian's knees.

Pitt went down hard, his rifle discharging in the trees. The sound was covered by the rumble of thunder, the muzzle flash by the gouting flames behind them.

The Missourian went down and Morgan slammed his fist into his face, all of the desperate force he could muster behind the blow. The man lay still beneath him and Morgan took the gunbelt from around his hips, the Winchester from his limp hand.

"Come on," Shell said, pulling Jean to her feet.

"Is he dead . . . ?"

"No. Don't worry about a man like that. You worry about your skin, you hear me?"

"Where are we going?"

"Nowhere if you don't keep quiet and keep your head down. You stay with me, you hear? And keep quiet!"

She nodded obediently. There wasn't much of Jean's old fiery spirit left on this cold and savage night.

Morgan knew where the horses were and he circled that way through the oaks, expecting resistance. By now the camp would be alerted and the first thing to be done would be to throw a guard around the corral.

Maybe not, maybe with luck . . . his heart sank.

He could see the two men—no, three. The lightning showed another man along the far rail, posted against the gate. Three men guarding the horses, and beyond was the bunkhouse, alight now as men dressed hurriedly, grumbling, cursing, and the rain fell down in a cold wash.

"What now?" Jean asked, clinging to his arm. "What can we do? He'll kill us!" Her voice rose to a shriek audible even above the hammering staccato of the rain. Morgan clamped his hand over the woman's mouth.

"Quiet! Just keep it quiet. Everything will be all right," he hissed in her ear. How it was going to be all right, Morgan didn't know. He was afoot against fifty armed men with fifty miles to go to safety. "All right?" He asked her that softly and he saw her head bob. He squeezed her shoulder and started toward the corral. He was going to have a horse. Two if possible. Without them he was dead anyway.

He left the girl in the trees and started toward the corral. He would have to take one guard out, possibly two. Then inside the corral, bringing two horses—the first two at hand-over the poles. It was a very uncertain proposition.

Morgan moved along the perimeter of the trees, keeping to the shadows, but the time came when he had to cross the twenty yards of open space between him and the nearest man. It should have been simplified by the dark and rain, but on this night the lightning was almost continuous, the flames from the burning house still danced high. The guards would be ready to shoot at anything that moved.

Shelter crouched now, steeling himself to make that last dash, to fire left, taking the first man, then right, at the man near the gate . . . there was something familiar about that one, and something about the one near at hand that he knew.

Morgan got to his feet. He had as much chance brassing it out as going in shooting. He walked across the empty space, rifle in his hands and Alvin Shore came alert, intent as he saw the tall man within a few strides of him.

"Johnny!"

"That's right, kid."

"You can't . . ." he stuttered. "They said you were a lawman of some kind."

"Did they? And you want to tangle with me now, do you?"

"I didn't . . ." the stuttering wasn't getting any better. Alvin had seen the tall man at work and he knew damn well he wasn't man enough to take him on.

"I want two horses, Alvin. Is that Blocker over there? I thought so. Nervous Ed?" Shore nodded. "I want two horses, my man. It's the killing time, Alvin. It's come real sudden. I don't have time to wait around. Why don't we get five horses out of there and you boys vamoose. It's that or fight me—I told you—I don't have time to wait and debate it."

For a moment Shelter thought the kid would draw and fire. Obligation, what he thought was obligation, seemed to gnaw at him. But he hadn't the steel to be an outlaw, hadn't the heart to face down a man like Shelter Morgan and he knew it.

In ten minutes the three new recruits were on their ponies and riding south, and Shelter Morgan with the woman at his side was mounted and high-tailing it out of the valley where the night riders searched the dark trees and the burning house, where the dead thing lay settled to cold ash.

They met the vigilantes at the head of the trail.

17.

"Just hold up there or die!" the voice of Lewis Decatur boomed out and Shelter reined in, grabbing the bridle of Jean Waltham's skittish mount.

"We're sitting tight," Shell called back. There was no answer for a minute and then the black-clad men came forward from out of the rain, fifty strong, all armed, all intent on deadly vengeance.

"Forsberg? Is that you?" Decatur asked uncertainly.

"It's me, but the name's Morgan. Shelter Morgan. I've got Jean Waltham with me and some bad news for you."

"Bad news?" The big man rode his horse up beside Shell. The horse reared and blew in the rain. Water glistened on Decatur's dark slicker and on his horse. It ran from his hat brim. His broad face was deeply grooved with determination. "What could be worse than the things that have already happened to me? My son dead . . ."

"Gloria. Gloria's dead," Shelter told him bluntly.

"Gloria . . ." Decatur nodded his head. He seemed to have known somehow. "She was bad. She was bad and very strange. Who did it?" His eyes lifted sharply and stared through the rain at Morgan who sat hatless before him.

"Bill Waltham."

"All right. You two get out of the way," Decatur said. "We're going through. I mean to finish the night riders off for good and all."

"I'm not moving," Shelter said.

"You're moving, by God, or we'll trample you down into the mud!"

"I'm going with you. There's no other way. I have to see Bill Waltham's dead body."

Jean just sat there listening. Her thoughts could have been a thousand miles away. Shelter hoped they were. It couldn't have been pleasant to think about Bill, to hear men plotting his death.

"I'll have some people escort the lady home," Decatur offered.

"The hell you will!" Jean flared up. "I don't want any help from you, Mr. Decatur. Who do you think you are anyway? You're responsible for much death and pain as well. Yes, you. You're not a lot better than the night riders, do you know that? You sit and think about it some dark night, think that maybe you've paid a fitting price for what you've done. Now get the hell out of my way. I'm going home." She hesitated. "You, Shelter Morgan, I'd like to thank you, but I can't. You'll kill Bill if you can. Maybe he needs it, I don't know, but I won't thank you for it. Don't bother coming by the ranch. I don't care to see you again either."

She slapped her horse with her reins and it leaped forward, crowding past the slicker-clad vigilantes and their mounts. Shell watched her until the rain and the night swallowed her up.

"Well?" he asked Decatur at length.

"Well," Decatur responded grimly, "there's still a job to do. Here," he fished in his saddlebags and brought out an old rain slicker. "We're all wearing these, and if a man wasn't . . . well, he might get himself shot. One thing, Morgan—Bill Waltham is my meat. I want him personally."

"We'll see about that when the time comes. I figure I've been chasing him a hell of a lot longer than you have, Decatur."

"I don't mean to stand arguing."

"No. Let's go on down and give them a little bit of hell."

For once the two men agreed on something. Decatur lifted his hand and the long columns of dark cavalry moved through the pass toward the final bloody showdown.

As they started down the grade the body of men seemed to gather momentum on its own, to charge forward eagerly, to roll down the slope like a dark wave of retribution. By the time they hit the flats they were riding at a run, and their guns began to speak as the first targets presented themselves.

Answering rifles flashed from the bunkhouse, from the corral, from the oaks. Shelter rode low across the withers, ignoring it all. He had no wish to slaughter the night riders, to side with the vigilantes. He had a feeling there wasn't much right on either side.

He was there for one purpose, for one purpose alone.

He wanted Bill Waltham and he wouldn't be cheated out of him. A night rider popped up in front of Shelter as he rounded the corner of the smoldering main house and Shell thrust out his Colt, triggering off square into the face of the outlaw. The man was yanked back by invisible strings, his face exploding and Shelter rode on, seeing the mad fireflies of the gun battle dance through the night. He hoped that the three men he had ridden in with had gotten out. They were still young enough to learn, to deserve a second chance.

Ahead through the trees Shelter saw two mounted men fleeing. It didn't have to be, but from the way they were dressed, from the horse the one man rode, that big roan he had ridden when Shelter had accompanied him to the valley . . . damn it, it was! The Missourian and Bill Waltham riding hell for it. Shelter stung his mount with his spurs and leaned low across the withers, urging it to full speed, pleading with the horse to put him within gunshot range for one final, killing bullet.

The two horsemen had vanished, however. Vanished through the trees, riding flat out toward the western end of the valley, away from the pass. There was another way out then, and if Morgan didn't stay close on their heels he was going to lose them. In the rain and dark he wasn't going to find a narrow trail leading out of the night riders' stronghold.

He was out of the trees now. Behind him the gunfire sounded like strings of firecrackers popping. The rain hammered down. He had to halt the horse he rode—he'd lost them! Damn it all to hell, they were gone.

Gone where? Morgan peered around him, seeing only the jumble of rocks to his right, the little quick-running rill to his left racing down toward the oaks, and ahead the sawtooth mountains illuminated once and once again now by sputtering lightning which struck low.

They hadn't gone into the ground. "The rocks then," he told himself. It was the only possibility. Was there a trail up through that devil's playground of boulders and slabs of granite? Shelter rode nearer, lifting his eyes to the impossible tangle of rock.

If there was a trail there it could wind up to the hills beyond. If . . . he saw nothing, nothing at all. Shell swung down from his horse and began to walk very slowly, peering at the rain-soaked earth, searching for some small sign of passing horses. It was impossible in the rain and the darkness, and now the two men he had been pursuing had been gone for long minutes.

He might have been alone in all the world just then. The firefight behind him was screened out by the night and the storm. Waltham and the Missourian were nowhere to be seen and Morgan had small hope now of finding them at all.

And then he saw it.

Upward winding, narrow. A black thread of a trail leading into the jumbled rocks. By the flicker of lightning he saw it clearer now. Yes, by God, that just might lead somewhere. Morgan started his horse up the trail and twenty feet on he saw with certainty that his wasn't the first horse up the trail on that night.

There was a little step in the trail and where a horse had scrambled up it the mud was grooved with the effort of hoofs. Shell smiled grimly in the darkness. He rode on more swiftly, left and then right through the rocks, ever ascending, his Colt locked into his hand as the storm drove down, the wind, the rain, the thunder and lightning, the jumbles of madly stacked boulders making a nightmare of the search.

The rock bounded down onto the trail in front of him and Morgan threw himself from his horse. The rock fell and was followed by the close explosion of a rifle. Morgan's horse reared up against the dark sky. The rifle from the rocks spoke again and Shelter, who had been waiting for the muzzle flash, fired in return.

He heard the scream of agony even above the wind

and rain. And then the man toppled forward, sliding face first down the rocks to lie on the trail still and dead.

"Tough luck," Shelter said. He turned the Missourian over with his toe. The South had lost another soldier.

Shelter's horse was gone, panicked into flight. Shell stood there now, back pressed to the massive boulder behind him, looking up the trail.

Why had the Missourian stayed behind? If there was a trail ahead that led up into and through the mountains, why hadn't both men gotten the hell out of there?

The answer might be that the trail led no such place. That it went into the rocks and dead-ended. It was a good guess. The two of them could hide out there until the battle below was over. No one would follow them up here—the rain would have obliterated any sign of passage in another hour.

"You're in here, you bastard," Shelter said. "I know damn well you are."

He started forward, not liking the set-up, being trapped below, not seeing a way up onto the rocks, although there had to be one if Pitt had gotten up there. The rain was driving, cold enough to chill Shelter to the bone, heavy enough to screen off all vision an arm's length in front of his face. He crept up the trail, feeling his way, eyes moving, searching. He was a primitive thing come a-hunting and his quarry was there. He knew he was there now. He could smell him, feel him. He *knew*.

He came up out of the ground. Had he been lying there, Indian style, covered with earth and brush? Or was he just emerging from hell, a twisted, killing demon rising shrieking from the bowels of the earth?

The gun was in his hand. The silver-mounted Colt. The beautifully engraved symbol of death, and Bill Waltham shouted some obscenity as he thrust it out before him as his mud-streaked face opened wide in a demon-curse, his eyes wide, his hair washed down around his ears.

He fired and he missed. He fired and the answering bullet took him in the throat. He fired and Shelter's second bullet followed the first, ripping into the heart of the demon, stopping the heart, letting the black bile that Bill Waltham had for blood flow from the cavity of his body and stain the mud briefly before the rain washed it away, cleansing the earth.

Waltham jerked and then lay still, contorted with death. The silver Colt lay inches from his fingers, his curved, white, dead fingers.

Morgan leaned back against the rocks and then crouched down. He stayed there, gun dangling between his knees, the rain pounding down over him. He stayed there watching the night, the storm and the silver Colt for hour upon hour upon hour. There wasn't enough rain to wash it all away, there just wasn't.

"Sure you got a cold, you crazy man," Lola said. Her room was warm. Her bed was soft. The rain outside still fell. "Sitting out in the rain all night? Are you crazy as I think?"

"Not much," Shelter answered. "Look at where I am."

"Yeah, sure. Now."

Lola came to him. She was naked and beautiful, her glorious breasts bobbed and swayed as she crossed the room to throw back the sheet and climb in with Shelter Morgan.

"I told you to stay with me," Lola Allison said. "No—you want to make a war. What was it, something to do with the night riders?"

"Something to do with them, yes."

"They hanged them all yesterday, those that came in alive. The circuit judge listened for ten minutes and sentenced them to hanging."

"Yes," Shell answered, snuggling against Lola's shoulder. Her lips were searching and warm. Her hand rested on his bare hip. Shell sniffed. He had gotten a cold. It was ridiculous when he thought about it. He wasn't planning on thinking about it. He was busy thinking about Lola.

"What's that lump?" Lola asked, grunting as she lifted her body and shifted it.

"That's all me, darlin'."

"Yes, I don't think so. Christ, a gun!" she said with revulsion.

"Back under the pillow with that, Lola."

"What do you need this for?" With disgust she handed him the revolver, holding it with two fingers. "You got all the gun you need down here."

She smiled as her hand found the gun and began to work up a good load. She lay against him, straddling him, her lips roaming across his throat and jawline, ear and temple.

Morgan's eyes were closed when the door burst open, but his reaction was swift and deadly. He rolled Lola to the floor where she landed roughly on her butt, her eyes wide with shock and incomprehension. Shelter never saw that.

He saw only the slender pale-haired man in the doorway, the sneer on the Preacher's lips, the big blue Colt in his hand.

Morgan's hand was already out from under the pillow, and he was moving. As he rolled left the Preacher triggered off and his .44 bored a smoldering hole in the mattress where Shell had been a split second before.

Shell was on the floor now, on one knee, and he fired

from that position, coming up to his feet as his first shot tagged the Preacher and drove him back against the wall.

Lola screamed and Morgan shot the Preacher again. He spun toward the bureau, knocked the water pitcher and bowl to the floor to break into a hundred fragments, tried to lift his Colt and found that he couldn't. It was an anvil in his hand and before him stood the tall man, his blue eyes mocking, the gun in his hand curling smoke.

"You're not so much," the Preacher managed to say, and then he buckled up and went to the floor to lie still, his blood slowly spreading, staining the floor maroon.

Shelter turned to Lola who came shuddering into his arms. The hotel manager was at the door, his eyes wide.

"What . . . ?" he gawked at the dead man, at the naked couple across the room.

"Get me another room," Shelter demanded. "I want it now."

"Yes, sir." The manager blinked three times mopped his perspiring forehead and took off at a clicking, short-gaited run.

"You all right?" Morgan asked Lola, sweeping the hair back from her forehead to kiss her.

"Yes. Sure. Morgan, you crazy man! Who the hell is this friend of yours?"

"A little man with a crooked seam in his brain, that's all. But he was no friend."

"No? You got more friends around? More going to shoot up the place?"

"None."

"No enemies?" she asked with a tiny grin. Shelter kissed her nose.

"No more friends, no enemies. Just you, Lola."

"Okay then. Let's move. Get! Grab up my wrapper, will you? Here's your boots. Out! Out! Call that manager and tell him my nerves are shot to hell. Get a bottle of champagne up here, okay. New room! Hot bath. Take me a week of screwing to recover. Let's go, Morgan. No more excuses—no cold, no guns, no funny men with white hair, boy. This time you get down to work and take care of a woman who needs some taking care of."

She walked out holding her clothes in front of her in a bundle. She walked out, traipsing down the hallway, her naked buttocks flexing and dancing, stalking toward the new room at the end of the hall where the manager stood gaping. Morgan wasn't far behind. And if the people in the hallway wanted to stare at him, let them. His thoughts were on the work that lay ahead of him, and from the looks of things that was going to be quite a chore.

THE NEWEST ADVENTURES AND ESCAPADES OF BOLT
by Cort Martin

#10: BAWDY HOUSE SHOWDOWN (1176, $2.25)
The best man to run the new brothel in San Francisco is Bolt. But Bolt's intimate interviews lead to a shoot-out that has the city quaking—and the girls shaking!

#11: THE LAST BORDELLO (1224, $2.25)
A working girl in Angel's camp doesn't stand a chance—unless Jared Bolt takes up arms to bring a little peace to the town . . . and discovers that the trouble is caused by a woman who used to do the same!

#12: THE HANGTOWN HARLOTS (1275, $2.25)
When the miners come to town, the local girls are used to having wild parties, but events are turning ugly . . . and murderous. Jared Bolt knows the trade of tricking better than anyone, though, and is always the first to come to a lady in need . . .

#13: MONTANA MISTRESS (1316, $2.25)
Roland Cameron owns the local bank, the sheriff, and the town—and he thinks he owns the sensuous saloon singer, Charity, as well. But the moment Bolt and Charity eye each other there's fire—especially gunfire!

#14: VIRGINIA CITY VIRGIN (1360, $2.25)
When Katie's bawdy house holds a high stakes raffle, Bolt figures to take a chance. It's winner take all—and the prize is a budding nineteen year old virgin! But there's a passle of gun-toting folks who'd rather see Bol in a coffin than in the virgin's bed!

#15: BORDELLO BACKSHOOTER (1411, $2.25)
Nobody has ever seen the face of curvaceous Cherry Bonner, the mysterious madam of the bawdiest bordello in Cheyenne. When Bolt keeps a pimp with big ideas and a terrible temper from having his way with Cherry, gunfire flares and a gambling man would bet on murder: Bolt's!

Available wherever paperbacks are sold, or order direct from the Publisher. Send cover price plus 50¢ per copy for mailing and handling to Zebra Books, 475 Park Avenue South, New York, N.Y. 10016. DO NOT SEND CASH.

FORGE AHEAD IN THE SCOUT SERIES
BY BUCK GENTRY

#10: TRAITOR'S GOLD (1209, $2.50)
There's a luscious red-head who's looking for someone to lead her through the Black Hills of the Dakotas. And one look at the Scout tells her she's found her man—for whatever job she has in mind!

#11: YAQUI TERROR (1222, $2.50)
The Scout's rescue of a lovely and willing young lady leads him into the midst of a revolution. Even with battles raging around him, Eli proves to her once again that a hard man is good to find!

#12: YELLOWSTONE KILL (1254, $2.50)
The Scout is tracking a warband that kidnapped some young and lovely ladies. And there's danger at every bend in the trail as Holten closes in, but the thought of all those women keeps the Scout riding hard!

#13: OGLALA OUTBREAK (1287, $2.50)
When the Scout's long time friend, an Oglala chief, is murdered, Holten vows to avenge his death. But there's a young squaw who's appreciation for what he's trying to do leads him down an exciting trail of her own!

#14: CATHOUSE CANYON (1345, $2.50)
Enlisting the aid of his Oglala friends, the Scout plans to blast a band of rampaging outlaws to hell—and hopes to find a little bit of heaven in the arms of his sumptuous companion . . .

#15: TEXAS TEASE (1392, $2.50)
Aiding the Texas Rangers, with the luscious Louise on one side and the warring Kiowa-Apache on the other, Eli's apt to find himself coming and going at exactly the same time!

Available wherever paperbacks are sold, or order direct from the Publisher. Send cover price plus 50¢ per copy for mailing and handling to Zebra Books, 475 Park Avenue South, New York, N.Y. 10016. DO NOT SEND CASH.